No, it wasn't possible!

The man had never said he was a surgeon! He had no right to be, not here at the District. Not here, disturbing her fragile peace of mind. . . Recollecting herself, Claire managed a faint, 'Good morning, Mr Colby. Is there anyone in particular you wish to see?'

If Claire had hoped for some personal response, she was to be disappointed. *This* John Colby was a far different man from the scruffy, bare-chested Apollo she had found in Martin's garden.

Dear Reader

This month we complete Margaret O'Neill's quartet with TAKE A DEEP BREATH, based around the accident and emergency department. We go to Australia with Lilian Darcy in NO MORE SECRETS, where the need to conceal Thea's romance with Joe leads to problems, and introduce a new Australian author in Meredith Webber, whose HEALING LOVE takes us to a burns unit in India — Leith and Gabe are fascinating people. We round up with TILL SUMMER ENDS by Hazel Fisher — warm thoughts as we move into spring!

The Editor

Hazel Fisher was a late entrant into nursing and was briefly a general nursing student before deciding on psychiatry. She worked as a mental nurse for several years before writing full-time.

Having lived in East Sussex all her life, she admits that most of her plots come when she's doing the household chores! She enjoys writing medical romances as they provide much needed escapism — for her as well as the readers!

Recent titles by the same author:

TOMORROW IS ANOTHER DAY
CAROLINE'S CONQUEST

TILL SUMMER ENDS

BY

HAZEL FISHER

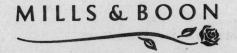

MILLS & BOON LIMITED
ETON HOUSE, 18–24 PARADISE ROAD
RICHMOND, SURREY, TW9 1SR

FOR MAM, WHO NEVER STOPPED CARING

First published in Great Britain 1994
by Mills & Boon Limited

© Hazel Fisher 1994

Australian copyright 1994
Philippine copyright 1994
This edition 1994

ISBN 0 263 78477 0

Set in 10 on 10 pt Linotron Times
03-9403-65518

Typeset in Great Britain by Centracet, Cambridge
Made and printed in Great Britain

CHAPTER ONE

CLAIRE SHAW absently pushed her fingers through her short, glossy brown hair, leaving it more in disarray than ever. So, Martin Medhurst was returning to Hemsley Green.

She turned to her cousin, Suzanne Arden, who was eyeing her speculatively. 'Just because the Medhursts are coming back, it doesn't mean Martin will be with them. It isn't logical,' Claire pointed out. 'He and his wife. . .' she hesitated; how difficult it was to say the word 'wife' now '. . .will stay in Suffolk, surely? Yes, of course they will!' she finished, and Suzanne chuckled, before stretching languorously.

They were in the living-room of the rather tumbledown house they shared in the Sussex village of Hemsley Green, some three miles or so from the resort town of Elmleigh, where Claire was a staff nurse at the District Hospital. The elegant and reed-slim Suzanne was stretched out limply on the settee, suffering from the sudden heatwave as much as Claire herself.

'That was your "Nurse must be obeyed without question at all times" voice, Claire, darling! You can't fool me—*I* know what Martin meant to you. And yes, I do think he's coming back to the manor—*sans* wife. Why not?' Suzanne helped herself to a chocolate and munched contentedly, while Claire surveyed her for a moment, a frown marring her high, smooth brow. The news about Martin had thrown her, and she wasn't sure whether to be glad or sorry.

Wandering restlessly over to the French windows, Claire stood gazing at the overgrown garden at the rear of the house. Flowers had been in short supply this year, but now, in early July, the weeds were still healthy, and it looked as if another all-day weeding session was overdue. Apart from the weeds, parched

lawn stretched as far as she could see and that, too,
needed attention, if only to chop off the heads of the
daisies, which seemed to thrive without water.
Suzanne had nicknamed it all the 'the jungle' and she
wasn't far wrong, Claire reflected with a rueful smile.
She wasn't far wrong about Martin, either. It was
typical of Suzanne to penetrate the chink in her
armour, though her cousin always did so with the best
of intentions.

True, Martin had once meant a lot to her, but that
was over now. Quite over, Claire assured herself,
memory of light brown eyes, an easy charm, an
infectious laugh coming back to remind her of just how
much he had meant. To be perfectly honest, and Claire
always tried to be, she had been head over heels in
love with him. Both of them had lived in Hemsley
Green all their lives, he in the manor house, she in the
doctor's house near by. Her widowed father had then
been the only GP in the village, and it seemed to
Claire that she had spent as much of her childhood at
the manor as she had at home. Memories of her late
father consisted mainly of scrawled notes left on the
mantelpiece explaining that he had been called out
and couldn't say when he would return. And one day
he hadn't returned. The police said he'd gone to help
at a road accident and been struck, in the poor light,
by another car.

Suzanne had been working abroad then, so the
Medhursts had taken the teenage Claire under their
wing, and she supposed she and Martin had been
thrown together too much. Then, suddenly, it was all
over. By then she had begun her nurse training, and
her awkward shifts at the hospital had clashed once
too often with the plans Martin had carefully laid in
advance; she simply wasn't available when he needed
her. Later, it was Martin who was always booked up,
had a meeting he simply mustn't miss, a legal conference he simply must attend.

Then had come the shock announcement in the
Hemsley Weekly News: Martin was marrying a girl
he'd met at one of those conferences. A 'whirlwind

romance', the paper had called it. Exit one broken-hearted nurse. Claire moved restlessly at the window, the memories still having the power to hurt her. She and Martin hadn't been engaged, no promises had been made, yet she'd had good reason to suppose he cared as much for her as she did for him. Words of love had come easily to Martin's lips. Too easily, she saw now. The only difference between them was that she had meant those delightful words 'I love you'.

Somehow she had survived, got on with her absorbing career, gained her prized registration certificate. Now, at twenty-three, she was a staff nurse in the surgical unit, and she wasn't about to let Martin upset her life again. Martin was in the past, and that was where he could stay!

But he's free, a little voice whispered. You knew it wouldn't last, that hasty marriage. If he isn't divorced, he's on the brink of it. He must have a good reason for returning to Hemsley Green. . . *He isn't coming back because of me*. Claire almost spoke the words aloud, but bit them back in time. Suzanne was a dear, but once she put her matchmaking mind to the problem anything could happen, even though she had never liked Martin.

As if to prove her right, Suzanne chuckled again. 'Just suppose, my dear, that Martin has belatedly discovered your true worth! Just suppose he's coming back ——'

'Just suppose it's time for lunch,' Claire said firmly, her expressive sapphire eyes hidden from her cousin's perceptive gaze as she made her way through to the kitchen at the side of the old house. 'Shall we have frozen steak pie or frozen fish fingers? You choose,' she called out once she had inspected the almost empty freezer. She gave a wry smile. This was what came of leaving Suzanne to do the shopping.

The manor house was situated at the northern end of the village, reached by a narrow, pot-holed lane which ran by the church. Once upon a time, Sussex roads had been famous — or infamous — for their dreadful condition, often becoming impassable in the winter, with the heavy wealden clay water-logged enough to stop an army. In summer the roads had formed a kind of dust-bowl, and Claire reflected that nothing much had changed, as she cycled along the lane towards the manor a few days later. Now the dusty lane seemed narrower than ever, with vegetation encroaching from the verges, and overhanging trees momentarily blotting out the sun.

It was still hot, and Claire was glad of the slight breeze caused by the movement of her cycle. It wasn't enough to stop her feeling overheated, though, and even the skimpy T-shirt and shorts she wore were too much. A bikini might have been better, but no doubt it would have caused the village elders to raise a brow or two!

Smiling at the thought, Claire continued on her way towards Martin's home. His grandparents had bought the house in the 1930s and had deliberately kept it as it had been in Edwardian times when it was in its heyday. People had come from all over the country then to attend the lavish house-parties, and once even the King himself had been a guest.

Martin's mother had insisted upon a few modern refinements, such as twentieth-century plumbing and central heating, but by and large the manor remained the same. Over the years the land had gradually been sold off, and now the family owned only a few cottages in the village. On Martin's marriage, nearly three years ago, his parents had let the property and retired to Spain. Now the Hemsley Green grapevine was throbbing with the news: the family were coming back. And Martin? Ah, thought Claire, if only I could be sure!

She stopped outside the house, leant her cycle against the open wrought-iron gates, then paused, uncertain what to do next. It wasn't like her to be unsure of herself, not the capable Staff Nurse Claire Shaw, yet she could hardly cycle up the drive to question the housekeeper about the Medhursts' movements. That would certainly keep the grapevine in fuel for days! True, she had known Mrs Taylor all her life, but what excuse could she offer for this unexpected visit? No, it would be better to do nothing, wait and see whether Martin sought her out.

Having decided that discretion was the better part of valour and that she had been a fool to come this far, Claire was just about to remount her bicycle and return home when a high-pitched yapping came faintly to her ears. It seemed to be coming from deep within the shrubbery which covered most of the front garden. The people who had rented the house were gone now, and, as far as Claire knew, none of the staff owned the small, yappy type of dog.

It was really none of her business, she felt, but the yapping, which had stopped momentarily, began again, interspersed this time with a heart-rending wailing. Abandoning her cycle, Claire ran towards the sound, thinking the animal might have its fur caught in a bush. The summerhouse would be a good vantage point, she decided, and this large octagonal building was reached most quickly by scrambling through a hole she found in the privet hedge which had once been Mr Medhurst's pride and joy.

Reflecting that the family would find a number of unwelcome changes when they arrived home, Claire plunged on, through the hedge, along an overgrown path reminiscent of their own wild garden, then past the greenhouse and kitchen garden. Here things were in better order, and she took a short-cut past neat rows of runner beans. Then, as she approached the dilapidated summerhouse, she saw the dog, a diminutive Yorkshire terrier, struggling to pull itself free from a wild blackberry bush.

Claire spoke soothingly as she approached, holding out her hand in friendship for the dog to sniff. It was too frightened to do anything except struggle harder and whine piteously, but at length dog and nurse emerged triumphant. It had lost a clump of hair and Claire had sustained one or two minor scratches from the bush, but otherwise all was well. Gently she put the squirming dog down, then brushed her hair back in a weary gesture. She was hot, tired, and in urgent

need of a cool shower. Her hair was a mess, and the
sun had brought out a crop of freckles. Reflecting
wryly that in such a situation Suzanne would have
emerged looking as coolly glamorous as ever, Claire
was about to follow the dog to make sure it found its
owner when a firm masculine voice said, 'Stay,
Dandy!'

Her eyes darkened with anxiety. No, she couldn't
meet Martin yet! She wasn't ready! But the man who
emerged through the rose arbour wasn't Martin
Medhurst. Bare-chested and suntanned, this unshaven
man was taller than Martin, with hair of a dark
caramel-brown, and the bluest eyes Claire had ever
seen. But the smile was the same — warm, friendly,
charismatic — and her lips tightened. Whoever he was,
he was cast from the same mould as Martin, and his
charm was wasted on her. She was immune!

'Thanks for rescuing Dandy. I've been trying to
track him down — I didn't know about the black-
berries.' The husky-voiced stranger bent to stroke the
dog's head and examine its coat, while Claire watched,
face flushed, what Suzanne called her 'Nurse Good-
body' calm momentarily deserting her. Then she
pulled herself together, mentally counting to ten, than
another five to be on the safe side. Take things easy,
Staff. You've seen enough bare male chests in your
time — why should this one set you all a-flutter?

She coloured even more, suddenly aware of the
man's gaze, which swept dispassionately over her
scantily clad body. For a moment she wondered
whether he might be a new gardener, yet there was an
air of command about him oddly at variance with his
scruffy jeans, and trainers from which, Claire noted,
his toes were protruding!

'I'm John Colby, by the way.' The stranger put out
his hand and gingerly Claire took it. No, he was
evidently not a man of the soil, with his strong but
well-kept hands and clean fingernails. His grip was
firm and if Claire hadn't been far too practical for such
romantic nonsense she might have admitted that his
touch did strange things to her heartbeat.

'Claire Shaw,' she murmured, as he released her hand. 'I live in the village,' she hurried on, hoping that would serve as an excuse for her passing the manor. Being a stranger, he probably didn't know the lane petered out once it passed the house and that she couldn't possibly have been going anywhere else. Averting her eyes, she bent to stroke the Yorkie, who had evidently decided she was a true friend. A little pink tongue began licking her, then, to Claire's alarm, the man's hand shot out and gripped her wrist, turning her hand so that the scratches showed.

'Did Dandy do this?' He ran a finger across the faint scratches, and Claire shook her head, her pulse-rate accelerating madly.

'No! It was the blackberry bush — I'll wash it with antiseptic when I get home. Please don't worry,' she said, fright making her sound brusque. She attempted to pull her hand from his grasp, but was unsuccessful. Then that charming smile broke out again, amusement gleaming from rather sensuous blue eyes.

'I don't bite, Miss Shaw. Come up to the house — you can wash there.' He surveyed her for a moment. 'Yes, you do look a bit grubby,' he continued, and Claire gasped. But before she could think of a suitable retort he bent and picked up the dog, then glanced back as if waiting for her. 'Do you know the Medhursts?' he asked, as she found herself unwillingly strolling beside him. 'Martin, perhaps?'

The dog wriggled until he put it down, and this gave Claire time to compose herself. 'Martin? Oh, yes, I've known him for years,' she said airily. 'Why? He isn't returning as well, surely? I thought it was just his parents.'

'The whole family are coming back — for a while, anyway. I'm the advance guard,' John Colby explained, a frowning question in his eyes as he glanced down at her. 'I've known Hugh Medhurst for quite a while and they're putting me up until I can find a house to rent. I'll be working in Elmleigh,' he went on, that easy smile warming her.

Aware that he was probing, Claire merely nodded.

If he hoped she was going to explain where she worked
and what she did for a living, he would have to be
disappointed. And her relationship with Martin
Medhurst was none of his business, either, she decided
as she preceded him into the huge flagstoned kitchen.
There was, she noted in dismay, no sign of the
housekeeper.

'The Taylors are off for the day, so I'm the sole
occupant, I'm afraid.. Come through to the cloakroom,' he invited, and Claire reluctantly did as she
was bid, wondering whether she was being rash.

'They're only little scratches, really,' she protested,
ashamed of her cowardice. Of course there was
nothing frightening about the man, rather the reverse,
and it was sheer arrogance to think that he had designs
on her. 'I'll dab them with something at home. They
aren't dirty, and I've had my tet jab,' she went on, the
words spilling over themselves in their struggle to get
out. The sooner she explained all this, the sooner she
could be on her way. For, despite having assured
herself that this man's intentions were honourable, he
was rather dishy, and her pulse hadn't yet settled down
to its normal steady rate!

He chuckled, perhaps aware of her mental conflict.
'You're a first-aider, too, then?' was all he said, before
running a little water into the basin and adding antiseptic. He tood aside while Claire bathed the scratches,
which were scarcely visible, but he did, thankfully,
retreat to the doorway of the sizeable cloakroom. It
seemed a lot of fuss to make over nothing, but Claire
fought down her nagging suspicions.

She let the water drain out of the basin, then
surveyed herself in the oval mirror, not liking what she
saw. A hot and bothered young nurse gazed crossly
back at her, with a face flushed from the sun and
perhaps from the proximity of a devastatingly attractive man, hair awry and badly in need of a good
brushing, and, worse still, a T-shirt that she saw now
was too tight and emphasised her breasts rather too
much. Flushing even more, she rummaged in her bag
for a comb, then heard a soft 'tut, tut' behind her.

Before she could react, John Colby had rinsed a face flannel under the tap, then began gently and methodically to wash her face. Claire reacted instinctively, struggling to break free. 'Be still! You've got webs and dust on that pretty face. There.' He stepped back when he had finished, and silently handed her a soft towel. She gazed at it for a moment, nonplussed, then buried her face in it, attempting to dry her face and avoid his eyes at the same time. What a fool he must think her!

Then indignation overcame embarrassment, and she almost flung the towel at him. 'There was no need to wash my face. I *can* manage that, thank you!' she snapped. 'I'm not a child!' Claire knew she looked nearer seventeen than twenty-three, a fact which did nothing to soothe her ruffled feelings.

A low chuckle broke from him. 'No, you aren't a child, are you? I must need spectacles!' Then he was gone, and Claire watched his lean, athletic figure disappear in the direction of the kitchen.

She took a few deep breaths before finally ferreting out her comb and trying to bring some order to her wayward locks. She couldn't hope to do so to her wayward thoughts, though, and, breasts still heaving with emotion, she emerged from the cloakroom. It would be unpardonably rude to stalk off without a word, so, shrugging aside her annoyance, she hovered in the kitchen doorway, just as her benefactor was setting down a bowl of water for the dog.

'Like some coffee? Or there's fresh orange juice,' he offered, but Claire shook her head then glanced deliberately at her watch.

'Thank you, but I can't, I'm afraid. I really have to get on and——'

'You've suddenly remembered an urgent appointment, right? Or is it an immediate need to wash your hair?' he suggested. He was laughing at her! His lips parted to reveal even white teeth, and those mesmerising eyes were alive with laughter. Although undeniably handsome, his face wasn't without lines, and most of them were lines of good humour, Claire noted in those few seconds, her nurse's eyes observing without her really being aware of it.

Still acutely discomfited but determined not to show it, she murmured her thanks. 'I really *do* have to get on, though,' she added quickly, then raised her hand in farewell before turning and walking from the kitchen. The only thing spoiling her dignified exit was Dandy, who came running along beside her with a soft, squashy ball in his mouth, evidently intending that she should play.

Being unable to resist the appeal in those sensuous blue eyes, Claire pretended to steal the ball, while Dandy ducked and yapped happily, then—— No! Wishing she could break into a run, Claire at last reached the safety of the drive. What dog, she wondered, as she cycled away, had sensuous blue eyes? The heat must be doing extraordinary things to her usually nimble brain!

'Have the Medhursts really got a tall, dark and handsome stranger staying with them? Perhaps I ought to investigate.' Suzanne had prised *some* of the details out of Claire when at length she arrived home, hot and bothered from her cycle ride. Of course, it was only *some* of the details. Claire hadn't been about to describe the odd, tingling sensation as John Colby had clasped her hand, or the admiring expression in those intensely blue eyes. . .

'I didn't say he was handsome and he certainly isn't all that dark,' Claire hedged, as they sat on the patio the following evening. From time to time, they glanced at the jungle, which still clamoured for attention. Since Claire was just finishing a precious week off duty, her cousin had insisted that neither of them should do a stroke of work that wasn't essential. Weeding, they had unanimously decided, wasn't essential.

'You described him as a tall, lean man with blue eyes,' Suzanne went on, clearly not going to let the matter drop. 'You can't deny that. I immediately decided he must be handsome and dark. You would have said if he was fair-haired, wouldn't you?' Martin

Medhurst has fair hair, the tone of voice implied, but Claire ignored the question.

Instead she stretched out her long legs trying to catch what remained of the sun's rays. They had both spent the day in bikinis, but now Claire wore a pink caftan against the coolness of the evening, the skirt pulled back to make the most of the fresh air. The day after tomorrow she would be sweltering in nylons and duty shoes and she did not relish the prospect. Though in some ways it would be good to get back to the hospital, she mused. It was funny how nurses couldn't wait to go on leave, then spent part of that leave thinking about the ward and its personalities, wondering whether Mrs A had fully recovered from her op, or if Mr B's chest was better.

In Claire's case she wondered how Mrs C was coping. Wendy Clark had been admitted to Camber Ward, women's surgical, for investigations only the day before Claire went on leave. Since she suffered from periodic bouts of depression, her hospitalisation naturally worsened that condition. Claire knew her outside the hospital, as Mrs Clark also lived in Hemsley Green, and the last time Claire had seen her was in the village, when a buoyant Mrs Clark had assured her she was on top of the world, that her favourite son had been to see her, and everything in the garden was lovely.

Claire liked the woman, admired the way she had brought up five children practically single-handed after her husband left her. Mrs Clark was the first person she would greet on the ward, Claire decided, once the problems of the first handover were sorted out, though by now she might have been discharged.

When she returned to work, too, there would be a new consultant surgeon starting, a woman, and rumour had it that Miss Tania Wallace was a real tartar! True, lady surgeons had to be somewhat tougher than their male counterparts if they were to reach the dizzy heights of consultant, but probably Miss Wallace wouldn't be the ogre everyone dreaded. Claire could only hope. Her ward sister, Sister Whitelaw, was on

the point of retirement, so there would be other
changes in the section. Changes were always unsettling, no matter that they might be for the better, and
she was beginning to wonder if, now that Martin was
definitely returning, it was time for her to seek new
pastures, strike out in a different area. London,
maybe, like Suzanne.

She stole a sideways glance at her cousin who
looked, as always, absolutely glamorous. Suzanne's
caftan was one she had run up herself in those vivid
colours which set off her striking colouring. This one
had an electric blue background patterned with huge
red and saffron flowers. Claire, with her pale complex-
ion, couldn't have carried off such an ensemble, but
Suzanne, with her slightly golden skin, long blonde
hair and vivid green eyes, looked stunning. The
thought crossed Claire's mind that if John Colby were
to materialise at that very moment he wouldn't even
see Staff Nurse Shaw. Beside Suzanne, she faded into
the background.

Then, annoyed with herself for letting those eyes and
that smile disturb her concentration, Claire went on to
discuss their plans for the following day. It was, she
recalled, tomorrow that the Medhursts were expected
in Hemsley Green. The Medhursts — and Martin.

CHAPTER TWO

'Welcome back, Claire! Had a good holiday?'

Claire turned and waited as the short, plump figure of Staff Nurse Jill Murray caught her up. They were in the corridor which led from the admin offices to the rehabilitation unit. This was Monday morning at a quarter-past seven, and if anyone had that Monday morning feeling it was Staff Nurse Shaw. 'Yes, thanks. It made a break,' she murmured. 'I haven't missed anything exciting, I suppose?' Claire went on, without any real expectation. Nothing exciting ever happened at Elmleigh District Hospital. Rumour had it that, even if an earthquake suddenly shook Sussex, the senior nurses and doctors would wait until their monthly meeting before discussing it.

She was surprised, therefore, when Jill paused dramatically. 'We-ll,' she said, 'it doesn't really concern me, but I've been dying to tell you—she didn't turn up!'

There was no need to ask who 'she' was. 'Miss Wallace has changed her mind about joining ye olde Emleigh District, I presume?' Claire said with mock-solemnity, and Jill laughed.

'Something like that, only she had no choice, poor thing. Had some family bereavement—her husband, I heard. So she's taken a few weeks off. The grapevine's buzzing with it!'

'So we're without a consultant? Oh, well, Collingwood can cope. He's always telling Sister how good he is.' Gram Collingwood was the senior surgical registrar, expecting his first consultancy any minute and anxious that everyone should know it.

'No, not Gram! Wasn't I just telling you? You don't listen, Claire. I'll see you in the canteen—tell you all about it then. Are you first lunch as usual?'

At Claire's quick nod, Jill puffed her way to her

17

ward, while Claire, ignoring the stairs for once, took the lift to the surgical floor, hurried along two more corridors, then found herself once more on Camber Ward.

Surgical was arranged on an open-plan principle, and visitors often complained that the wards sprawled to such an extent that they never knew where one ward ended and another began. Although each section of Surgical had its own nurses' station, the sister's office was tucked away at the end of the ward, and relatives had been known to wander in bewilderment up and down the lengthy corridors seeking the reassuring sight of a nurse in the familiar navy blue.

Wondering whether she would ever be privileged to don that uniform but very much doubting it, Claire responded cheerily to the greetings from the Camber morning shift. She was popular with the other nurses who seemed to bear her no ill-will for her cherubic prettiness, her huge golden-lashed sapphire eyes, her neat figure, and legs that went on forever, as one besotted young houseman had once described them!

Suppressing a yawn, she tried to settle down behind Sister's desk to listen to the problems of the night. Since Sister Whitelaw wouldn't be on duty until nine, it fell to Claire to take the handover from the night nurse. After Suzanne's late-night party, though, she was feeling rather delicate, and concentrating on anything was going to be an effort this morning. Even Martin had been pushed to the back of her mind.

'Quiet night on the whole. Most patients slept well,' Bibi Bhunjun, the night nurse, intoned. 'Mrs Lister was discharged yesterday, and there are. . .yes, four patients you won't know: Mrs Russell, who's for cholecystectomy, two for exploratory surgery—Miss Attwood and Mrs Saunders, and an acute appendix, Mrs Wright. She was query peritonitis and that's what they found. Mrs Russell's gall-bladder op was cancelled once before because there wasn't a bed, and she's very anxious,' Bibi went on, before raising her eyes from the Kardex. 'Wendy Clark's still here. Investigations were mostly negative as you can see, but she had a problem with her bowels which we've cleared up. Enema given with good result, and she's had suppositories since — bowels open twice in the night. Advice given re diet, but you know what she's like, Claire. She's on lactulose at present, and she's due for discharge but she's as low as I've ever seen her. Mentally, anyway.'

'But she looked so well only a few weeks ago!' Claire exclaimed. 'I would have sworn she was genuinely happy when I saw her in the village.' Because her sister had died of cancer, Mrs Clark was inclined to magnify every symptom into a malignant growth, and the fact that she suffered from a long-standing depression didn't help.

'The test results are all in the case papers. Here.' Bibi passed Wendy's notes across the desk. 'Have a talk to her when you're settled in,' the night nurse went on. 'You were always her favourite. Oh, by the way, did you have a good holiday? The pleasant memory will soon fade, if you did,' she added sourly, and Claire's eyes widened.

'Oh — you mean because of Miss Wallace not coming? Yes, Jill Murray told me. So, are we left to the great Collingwood's tender mercies?' Claire didn't particularly like Gram, but better the devil you knew, she mused. He was kind to the patients, if a trifle aloof.

'If only we were! No, my dear, we've a new consultant. Just temporary until That Woman starts. And if you think Gram's difficult, you should try this one! He — ' Bibi broke off abruptly, her eyes opening wide in dismay, and Claire followed her gaze, then hastily rose, as did the other nurses, with much scraping back of chairs.

'Good morning, sir!' they chorused, as a tall, lean man materialised out of nowhere, or so it seemed to Claire's horrified gaze. She was rendered speechless for a moment, her usual poise deserting her as an embarrassed Bibi introduced her to the new consultant. It was John Colby!

No, it wasn't possible! The man had never said he

was a surgeon! He had no right to be, not here at the
District. Not here, disturbing her fragile peace of
mind. . . Recollecting herself, Claire managed a faint,
'Good morning, Mr Colby. Is there anyone in particular you want to see? We haven't finished the handover
yet;' she added with a smile. Hardly surprising, that,
since it wasn't much past seven-thirty, and everyone
knew consultants never appeared on the wards *that*
early.

If Claire hoped for some reponse, she was to be
disappointed. This John Colby was a far different man
from the scruffy, bare-chested Apollo she had found
in Martin's garden. Gone were the designer stubble
and casual clothes, and now she had a clear view of his
face Claire saw the forceful chin, the determined set
of his mouth. Those eyes were as blue as before,
although she wouldn't have been surprised if they had
changed to a steely grey. Oh, dear, she thought,
another Gram.

As if she had conjured him up, the registrar's long,
thin face and long, thin body appeared in the doorway.
Her only consolation was that Gram Collingwood
wouldn't like the situation any more than she did. But
she was wrong, for the registrar's eyes were fixed
earnestly upon John Colby and he appeared to be
hanging on the man's every word, perhaps hoping he
might pick up a few tips on how to behave when he
finally became a consultant!

'I thought we would take a look at Wendy Clark,
Staff Nurse,' Mr Colby said, his eyes surveying her
coolly. Almost as if, Claire thought, he had never
washed her face for her, never run his fingers gently
over those few little scratches, never ever *seen* her
before.

'Now? She probably hasn't bathed yet, and we've——'
she began, then stopped at Gram's loud gasp.

'Then hurry her up, please! We mustn't keep a
consultant waiting.' The registrar smiled oilily. 'We're
lucky to get Mr Colby at such short notice, you know.'

'Staff Nurse Shaw doesn't think so,' the said Mr

Colby commented, and Claire blushed. How right he was!

'Will you wait while Nurse sees what state Mrs Clark is in — or is there someone else you want to see first?' With an effort, Claire kept her voice steady. Her determined chin tilted a little. No, she would not be browbeaten by a consultant, however senior, and most certainly not by *this* consultant!

There was a gleam in the surgeon's eyes now which might have been appreciation. 'We'll wait in the day-room while you finish the handover,' he said softly, 'but please be quick, Staff — I've a busy day ahead.' The door closed on the two men, and Claire smiled grimly at her nurses while Bibi shrugged and raised her expressive eyes heavenwards.

'Perhaps we can finish now,' Claire suggested quietly, and within a few minutes all the necessary information had been passed from night staff to day staff. As Bibi had said, the night had been quiet, but that was a relative term in any ward. It didn't mean that no problems had arisen. Fortunately Camber Ward was full, as was generally the case, so the patients' sleep hadn't been disrupted by any emergency admissions. Although most patients had slept well, sleep was always difficult in hospital and one or two patients had spent a restless night, Wendy Clark among them. She was able to get off to sleep without trouble but suffered from early morning waking, and had lain awake since two o'clock, crying quietly. Nothing the nurses said or did seemed to help, and she took no interest in any of her fellow patients. Most of the ladies did, becoming almost as interested in their bed-neighbours' symptoms as they were in their own. They became protective of one another, generously sharing flowers, chocolates, tissues — and lurid details of their ops!

Gaynor Wingrove, in the next bed to Wendy, was a great one for handing out advice, but Claire rather thought Wendy might have been listening to a run-down of Gay's symptoms as well, and had begun to imagine she shared some of them. Despite Gay's major intestinal operation, she had become the life and soul of the ward and they would miss her when she was discharged. But apparently now she, too seemed disinclined to leave the hospital and was talking about seeing her MP.

Claire raised a brow. 'Why? If she's got a complaint against us, there's the usual procedure to follow. Did you explain that to her?'

'Oh, yes, Night Sister did that, but Gay's been reading some stuff in the tabloids about patients being turned out of their hospital beds too soon, and she's decided she wants another week here! With a waiting-list as long as your arm, *she* decides she'll take up a bed we desperately need! Mr Colby will sort her out, though,' Bibi added with satisfaction, and Claire silently agreed. Mr Colby looked just the type! Even without a shirt, she had thought there was a certain air of command about him, an expectation of being obeyed. Claire's mouth set in a firm line. Darn shirtless consultants!

Wondering why he needed to see Wendy so early, Claire sent a student in search of her, and was dismayed to learn that Wendy intended to spend the day in bed, and was determined not to be discharged. It was, Claire reflected, going to be One of Those Days!

She had met Gay Wingrove before going on holiday but most of the other patients were new, and she must introduce herself to them, Claire knew, but where to begin? Bed-curtains were being whisked back from beds as she approached those in the cubicle nearest the office, and all was bustle as nurses hurried about wheeling commodes, bringing in the vases of flowers that had spent the night outside the office, or finishing tidying those patients who couldn't manage for themselves.

Quickly Claire glanced down at her list, aware that a certain Mr Colby was deep in conversation with their pretty Finnish house-surgeon over by the nurses' station. Smilingly she approached Mrs Wright, the lady who had developed full-blown peritonitis. Evelyn Wright was in her late fifties but looked younger, with ash-blonde hair cut in an attractive style, and kind hazel eyes.

'I'm Staff Nurse Claire Shaw, Mrs Wright, and I'm in charge till Sister comes on duty. How are you?'

Mrs Wright pulled a face. 'Well, to tell you the truth, Nurse, I'm feeling a bit washed out. My old appendix has been grumbling on and off for ages but I just kept ignoring it, hoping it would go away! Then I got these awful pains, here. . .' She indicated the right side of her abdomen, low down. 'Then it seemed to spread all over and I got frightened, I don't mind telling you. Thought it was something serious, you know — the big C!' The patient managed a laugh, but Claire could see that the thought of a malignancy was still worrying her.

'What you ended up with was peritonitis, Mrs Wright,' Claire explained. 'That's sometimes a complication of acute appendicitis and it's where a membrane in the body, the peritoneum, becomes inflamed as well. That's why you've been in such pain since and needed those injections. Are you in pain at all now?'

Although the patient shook her head, Claire didn't believe her. Mrs Wright was, from the report, a lady who hated to be a nuisance or make a fuss. Unfortunately it was that type of patient who got less attention than those more demanding, Claire felt, as she walked briskly away in search of a couple of paracetamol.

She was just unlocking the drugs trolley in the clinic when she saw a movement and became aware that John Colby had followed her in. 'Busy, Miss Shaw?'

Claire swung round. The surgeon's smile was lopsided, attractive, once more the smile of Apollo, and Claire, flustered, almost dropped the keys. Retrieving them, she said, 'We're always busy on Camber, Mr Colby. Mrs Wright, the lady in bed one, is still in pain after her peritonitis, I think, though she denies it. I'm giving her something for it now, as she's written up for paracetamol p.r.n, then I'll get back to the ward. I need to introduce myself to most of the ladies — a week is a long time in Surgical!'

'True,' he acknowledged. 'Why didn't you tell me

you nursed here?' Arms folded, he leaned against the door, waiting.

Well! Who was he to ask that? 'For the same reason you didn't tell me you were a surgeon,' she replied sweetly, before carefully writing in the medication on Mrs Wright's card. Relocking the trolley with a flourish, she turned back to the grinning surgeon. 'You might have told me your symptoms, Mr Colby, and that would never do!'

'*Touché!* Though I'd be happy to listen to *your* symptoms any time, Staff Nurse.' Before Claire could recover, he was gone. Now what did he mean by *that?*

'He's having *breakfast* with my patients?' Sister Whitelaw sat back in her chair and glared at Claire a little later.

'Well, not now, Sister—we've finished breakfasts,' Claire said with a twinkle in her eye, but the ward sister wasn't in her usual jovial mood.

'Don't be facetious, Claire, you know what I mean! How did you come to allow Mr Colby to eat on the ward? You know we mustn't eat patients' food. It's a hanging offence,' the plump, grey-haired sister went on, her anger visibly subsiding. 'He's rather nice, isn't he? I had him in mind for Stella.'

'Stella?' Claire said faintly, unable to visualise the good-looking surgeon with the rather astringent Sister Pountney on men's surgical. 'He's married with a family, I expect,' she went on, and thought the older woman gave her a sharp look. Well, hadn't he spoken about looking for a house locally? If he were a bachelor, surely a flat would be sufficient?

'Don't believe all you hear, Claire. Now, did you have a good holiday? Fine, we can get down to work,' Sister went on without giving Claire time to speak. 'Give me a rundown on the patients—I was off yesterday and Stella was overseeing the ward,' she explained, and Claire understood: Stella Pountney had looked John Colby over and decided he was just what she wanted. Of course, it was none of her business, but Claire couldn't help thinking he deserved better.

None of the juniors was happy on Stella's ward and she—— Just in time Claire caught the trend of her thoughts. She would turn into a jealous harpy if she didn't watch out! Because her own romance had turned sour and Martin had decided he could do better for himself, that was no reason to have jealous thoughts about other women. If Mrs Colby ever wanted rid of her husband, then Stella was perfectly entitled to stake a claim.

The mesmerising John Colby had, indeed, break-fasted in the dayroom with those patients who were 'up'. That included Wendy Clark, since she was for discharge. Wendy had been persuaded to put on a dressing-gown, and, although she sat contentedly with Mr Colby at breakfast, she had merely picked at her food, and, once his attention was engaged with another patient, had slipped quietly out of the dayroom and would have returned to bed if Claire's vigilance hadn't prevented her.

Claire's lips curved into a smile as she recalled Gram Collingwood's expression when he learned he and his boss were to eat on the ward. 'But sir! We can't do that!' And when the consultant had enquired mildly why they could not, Gram had stammered, 'It's against hospital rules, sir. Hospital policy, you know. . .' His voice had trailed away and he had turned an uninter-esting beetroot colour as he'd apparently realised he shouldn't be lecturing a consultant on hospital policy. So both men had sat down with the patients, though they had eaten food sent up from the staff canteen. If Gram hadn't enjoyed the experience, the patients certainly had, once they were over their astonishment. A consultant actually unbending to sit and eat with them! Given that consultants at the District were treated as gods, some of the patients must have been surprised to learn that they actually *did* need to eat!

Now it was mid-morning, and the drinks trolley was just being wheeled away as Claire approached Dora Russell's bed. She had earlier met the patient, who was due to have her gall-bladder removed in the morning, but hadn't had time to fully answer her questions.

'Can I offer you a little tender loving care?' Claire asked with a cheery smile, and Mrs Russell returned the smile though she clutched anxiously at Claire's outstretched hand.

'It will be all right, won't it? You're sure they'll take me down tomorrow? Only when the operation was cancelled before, I got that uptight about it. Then Charles started. . .' Mrs Russell's voice trailed away. 'He can't bear to see anyone ill, you know. He's always been so fit himself that he doesn't understand how people *can* get ill or need an operation.'

'He might need one himself one day, then he'll know what it's all about, won't he?' Claire agreed, settling herself by the bed. 'Shall I run through the details of what you can expect afterwards; I know Mr Colby did but ——'

'What a handsome man! But is he a good surgeon? That's what matters, isn't it, Nurse? You hear tales about some of them. . .' Mrs Russell plucked at the sheet, then met Claire's gaze, and Claire saw the fear in her eyes.

'You can have every confidence in Mr Colby,' she said automatically. She'd had no experience of his operating technique, and, as Mrs Russell said, one *did* hear tales about certain surgeons. But John Colby was bound to be gentle, Claire just knew it. 'You won't have any breakfast in the morning,' she began, 'and one of the staff nurses will give you an injection to help relax you, and she'll close your bed curtains so you can sleep if you feel drowsy. Theatre will ——'

Mrs Russell raised a hand. 'Please don't! I'd rather not know,' she insisted. 'That nice consultant did tell me about a drain from the wound and I thought he said "tubes", but I don't want to know any more. Just leave me to rest, my dear.' She slid down in the bed, but Claire couldn't allow that.

'You needn't stay in bed, Mrs Russell. Perhaps you'd like to sit in the armchair by your bed? Your lunch will be in the dayroom so you'll need to get up then. Too much bed-rest causes complications,' Claire added firmly, as the patient seemed about to refuse.

Dora Russell made a moue, but eased herelf reluctantly out, Claire helping her into her stylish satin slippers. She was forty-nine but could have passed for thirty-plus, and Claire knew she took pride in looking good, peering into her hand mirror as if to reassure herself constantly that she looked younger than the others in the cubicle.

'You will come to see me again before you go off duty, won't you, Staff?' Mrs Russell was saying, as Claire settled her in the big chair. 'Sister did come over but she was called away, and there never seems to be a *trained* nurse about when you want one.' The patient sounded peevish but Claire ignored that. It might have been her usual behaviour but more likely it was apprehension about the coming operation. Some patients expressed their fear that way, complaining about minor, totally unimportant details because their minds couldn't face the real cause of their anxiety — going down to Theatre and being 'put to sleep'.

Having reassured Mrs Russell on that count, Claire went in search of their new learner, Nurse Baker. She was an attractive, well-meaning girl and popular with the patients, but seemed to have no confidence in her own abilities. A nurse's first ward was a strange and sometimes frightening place, Claire reflected, particularly in general surgery where anything could happen.

'Nurse! Come quick!' came the cry from one of the cubicles, and Claire ran in, to find Mrs Saunders gasping for breath before slumping forward in her chair. She was a huge, obese woman in for investigations, and Jackie Legg, the patient who had called out, was hovering over the armchair. 'I think she's a goner, Nurse Claire,' she said, while Claire, quickly assessing the situation, pressed the emergency button.

'Dial 3 for the crash team!' she called out to Nurse Baker, who was hovering, her eyes wide with horror. 'Hurry! Then get Sister.' If only the patient weren't so big! There was no possibility of getting her on to the bed before the crash doctors arrived, so the floor it must be, but first those few vital lungfuls of air. Every second counted in cardiac arrest because of the danger of permanent damage to the brain cells if they were starved of oxygen. All this passed through Claire's mind as she began her task. Mrs Saunders's face was ashen, lifeless, her lips becoming cyanosed, and after checking for and not finding a carotid pulse and making sure that the patient's tongue wasn't in the way Claire tilted Mrs Saunders's head back and lifted her chin to open up the airway. Then, pinching the woman's nostrils firmly, Claire took a deep breath, opened her mouth and sealed her lips around the patient's mouth before blowing air in gently but firmly.

Then Sister Whitelaw appeared, closely followed by John Colby and a tall, smartly dressed woman Claire had never seen before. Together they managed to get the patient on to the bed, after all, and Claire continued the resuscitation while the surgeon began closed cardiac massage, and Sister whisked the bed-curtains around them. The tall woman moved Claire to one side before quickly inserting an airway then 'bagging' air in that way, an artificial form of the 'kiss of life' that Claire had been performing on the patient.

The rattle of the 'red devil' heralded the arrival of the crash team, and Claire thankfully slipped outside the curtains while they set to work. Her task was over now and there were other patients who might need assistance, and certainly reassurance.

'Well done, Claire,' Sister approved. 'I was just saying to John what a good ward sister you would make, and now you've proved me right. Keep a cool head in an emergency, get your priorities right — that's all it takes.' Sister went back to Mrs Saunders's bedside, leaving a shaken Claire and an obviously frightened Student Nurse Baker.

'I was going to do some teaching, wasn't I?' Claire murmured before smiling reassuringly at the student, who was only a couple of years younger than Claire herself. 'Don't worry, we don't often get emergencies, and you coped well, Nurse. I'll run through the procedure with you later, when we're quiet again. Talk to

the patients in here, will you? Give them a bit of
TLC,' Claire suggested, and Nurse Baker darted away,
clearly relieved that she wasn't required to do anything
more demanding.

Despite Claire's prompt action and all their efforts,
it proved impossible to resuscitate Mrs Saunders, and
John left the cubicle, shaking his head slightly in
answer to Claire's enquiring look. 'I'm afraid not. She
had CCF anyway and could have gone at any time,
Claire. You did your best.' Briefly he laid his hand on
her shoulder. 'I'll see you in the office later. We have
a lot to discuss.'

A saddened Claire was left wondering what it was
they had to discuss. Then she straightened her
shoulders, repositioned her cap and tried to put the
woman from her mind. A death on the ward was
traumatic for the juniors a well as the other patients,
and time must be found for them to express their
feelings, but, for now, duty called.

Later, Claire made another unsuccessful attempt to
begin a teaching session, intending to broach the
subject of death and bereavement, but Sister Whitelaw
hove into view, smiling benignly.

'Ah, Claire, there you are. You've been bustling
about so much I can't keep track of you!' Sister was a
great favourite with her nurses as well as the patients,
and the ward wouldn't be the same without her larger-
than-life personality. And, Claire knew, Sister's retirement would leave a vacancy, one she had thought long
and hard about applying for. But how could a nurse
ever hope to replace someone like Sister Whitelaw,
particularly in an emergency situation, where her calm
manner was invaluable?

'Yes, Sister, here I am. Oh—what about Wendy?'
Claire raised an enquiring brow. 'I thought about
getting the student to help her pack, but is she definitely going tomorrow?'

'It's up to Mr Colby,' Sister broke in, lowering her
normally booming voice. 'He wants to make a special
study of a patient, and he's chosen Wendy Clark. I
expect she'll be allowed to stay on another day or two.

I told him you had the best rapport with her, so he suggests you and he get your heads together!' Sister went on, her eyes sparkling behind her spectacles, and Claire tensed. She didn't want to get her head together with Mr Colby!

'You know her better than I do, Sister,' she pointed out quickly. 'It's my first day back and I don't think I can tell our new consultant anything helpful. He can read the case notes, surely?'

'Sign of a bad doctor or nurse, reading case notes and not bothering with the patient herself — you know that as well as I do, Claire. I've had to speak to that junior about it. And she's been making sheep's eyes at my Mr Colby,' Sister went on, and Claire managed a wan smile.

'He's your Mr Colby now, is he? I'm ashamed of you, Sister! Anyway, I thought I might do some teaching on the ward before the lunches. You know you like us nurses to stay with the patients as much as possible,' Claire pointed out, and Sister looked scandalised.

'When a consultant asks to see a particular nurse, that nurse obeys — at the double, Staff Nurse.' She gave Claire a firm push in the direction of the office, and, feeling mutinous, Claire did as she was bid, wondering why Mr Colby wanted to make a 'special study' of a patient. She wasn't going to let him conduct research on *their* patients!

Prepared to do battle, Claire knocked firmly on the slightly open door of the ward office, then paused as she heard voices within. 'Come in, Nurse,' Mr Colby's deep voice invited, and she did so, pausing on the threshold, her gaze riveted upon the tall, slender woman who had assisted at the cardiac arrest. John Colby was leaning against the wall, arms folded defensively, a forbidding expression on his face.

'I'm sorry, sir, I didn't know you were busy. I'll come back later,' Claire said, itching to beat a hasty retreat, but this was to be denied her.

'No problem — Miss Wallace was just going.' His face relaxed into a smile as he turned towards the woman. 'Staff Nurse Claire Shaw, my dear. Staff Nurse, this is Miss Tania Wallace, your unit's new consultant. At least she will be, before long.'

'Good morning, Miss Wallace,' Claire said warily, her assessing gaze quickly taking in the warm smile on the woman surgeon's face, the almost shy way she offered her hand. Was *she* the ogre they had dreaded for weeks? From the look of her, she would be a considerable improvement on Mr Colby!

'John wants to make a special study of your pet patient, Staff Nurse, so I'll leave you to it. We'll meet again before too long. I——' Miss Wallace hesitated, before continuing, 'I had a bereavement, but I'm looking forward to joining the unit soon.'

With a smile for Claire she turned to go, and both Claire and John Colby hurried to open the door for her. To Claire's astonishment, he brushed his lips across his colleague's hair before ushering her out, then closed the door firmly. There was a sad smile on his face, then it faded abruptly.

'Miss Wallace and I are old friends. What you might call "intimate acquaintances",' he explained. 'I'm sorry you had to meet in such circumstances. Now—Wendy Clark. What can you tell me about her before I go delving into her case notes?'

His penetrating gaze caught Claire unawares, and she floundered for an instant, unable to bring her own thoughts back to the patient. Intimate acquaintances. . . Did that mean what she thought it did? 'Oh, yes, Wendy,' she murmured. 'When is Miss Wallace actually joining us?' she asked, surprising herself. Of course she had a right to know. The woman would be their own consultant, and, when Miss Wallace arrived, Mr Colby would go. That her interest in the lady doctor might be due to more than that Claire never paused to consider.

'Tired of me already?' That sensual smile was back on John Colby's face, and Claire was once more facing Martin, listening to his protestations of love, feeling the intensity of his gaze, catching her breath at the

passion she saw in his blue eyes. . . No! Martin had
brown eyes!

'Your face closed up then,' the blue-eyed one commented. 'That's a pity.' His expression was quizzical
now, and Claire fought down the anger, most of it
anger with herself. She hadn't been aware of any
movement, but now he was standing only a few inches
away, almost within kissing distance. If she put out a
hand she ——

Pulling herself together wasn't easy, but if she ever
wanted to become a ward sister she would have to
keep her mind firmly on her job — not let herself be
side-tracked by an undoubtedly attractive man with
more than twice the amount of charm he should have
been allocated! 'Did it?' she said stonily. 'I'm sorry
about that, sir. About Wendy ——' She hesitated, the
patient once more in the forefront of her thoughts.
'She's had four admissions to Camber over a period of
five years,' she stated. 'They're always for investigations but nothing is usually found, and she's been
prescribed l ——'

'Yes, yes, if I want a lecture on the subject, I can
give myself one,' the consultant said testily. 'What I
want is *your* opinion, your observations on her, your
gut feelings, if you want to put it like that.'

Startled, Claire met his gaze. There was nothing in
it now to which she could object, and she began to
relax. It was foolish of her to see Martin in the man,
and she had nothing to fear from him. Her sore heart
would not be exposed to further trauma. 'I really see
Wendy as a deeply unhappy woman, though I met her
recently in the village and she looked happy enough.
She had that "on top of the world" expression, but it
wasn't mania,' she said slowly, feeling her way through
the problem that was Wendy Clark, trying to see life
through the woman's eyes. What was it that had
brought her down to her present state? And was there
anything seriously wrong physically?

'Yes?' the surgeon said encouragingly, when Claire
hesitated.

'I keep thinking we may have missed something,'

she said, hurrying on in case he said, Rubbish, of course we haven't, as Gram had said just before she went on holiday, or, Aren't you being rather fanciful, Staff Nurse?, as their previous consultant had put it.

But this consultant didn't. 'Such as?' was all he said, but Claire shook her head.

'I'm afraid I don't know. It may be psychosomatic,' she suggested. During her training she had spent three months in the Elmleigh psychiatric unit, and found this extra knowledge very useful when confronted by patients like Wendy.

'The mind influencing the body. We shall have to see about Wendy, shan't we? You and I must work together on this,' John Colby said, smiling slightly.

Not sure she liked that idea, Claire murmured a polite, 'Yes, of course,' then was disconcerted by his husky chuckle.

'You would rather run a two-minute mile than work on anything with me, wouldn't you?' he said quietly. 'Now I wonder why?'

Before Claire could indignantly and untruthfully deny such a thing, he turned away, then yawned and stretched before rubbing the back of his neck as though weary, as he must be. Claire was reminded irresistibly of their earlier meeting. Once more she could see the grounds of Hemsley Manor, but this time it wasn't Martin Medhurst she saw, it was the bronzed torso of John Colby. Well, she wasn't about to make the same mistake again, wasn't about to fall for an insincere charmer. No matter what it cost, she would keep her stupid feelings under control, and not let herself be swayed by a pair of sleepy blue eyes!

CHAPTER THREE

CLAIRE saw that Jill Murray had saved a seat for her in the canteen, and she carefully carried her tray over to the table by the big window which overlooked the rear of the hospital. One or two patients from the psychiatric annexe were strolling about, enjoying the welcome sunshine, and Claire peered, turning her chair slightly so that she had a better view. Yes, it *was* Wendy Clark, talking to a man.

Despite Wendy's loudly declaimed intention of returning to bed for the day, they had managed to persuade her not only to dress but also to accept the fact that she was to be discharged in two days' time. Mr Colby saw no reason why she should have to languish in her nightwear if the tests were complete, and Claire couldn't fault that.

'Claire, hurry up and eat your meat and two veg,' Jill said, chuckling, 'the gravy's beginning to congeal!'

'Ugh, don't!' Claire stared down at her plate, wondering why she had bothered with a meal. Usually a morning on the ward gave her a tremendous appetite, but not this morning.

'Well, did you meet the charismatic Colby?' Jill demanded. 'Isn't he dishy? Of course, I've only seen him a couple of times, but Stella Pountney said he——'

'She would,' Claire broke in. 'She fancies him, I believe, though he's bound to be married.'

'Bound to be,' Jill agreed, spearing a chip and chewing carefully, 'although. . .' She shook her head. 'No, I mustn't repeat gossip,' she said, then giggled while Claire simmered.

'Gossip about what? Or whom?' she asked casually, and Jill waved her fork.

'Mustn't say. What I *will* say is that a certain consultant and a certain ward sister have been seen in Nona's actually having a cuddle!'

34

Nona's was a local nightspot. Claire had been there once with Martin, but the music was nothing special and the prices were beyond the reach of a mere nurse. 'What were you doing in Nona's, Staff Nurse Murray?' Claire asked, rapping her friend with her spoon.

'Dave took me for a special treat, but I'd had such an awful day that I sat there half asleep,' Jill confessed. 'Then I woke up, for who should come right by our table but Sister Pountney! And who was she with?'

'Mr Colby,' Claire said bleakly.

'Yes, that's right — and they were arm in arm. Then old Pountney snuggled up to him. You know how she is.'

'Yes.' Claire's voice was stony, but Jill appeared not to notice as she went on enthusiastically describing the scene at the club.

'Of course I sat up then and started taking nourishment, as we say. They danced together the *whole* evening, Claire! He's got a lovely smile, hasn't he? Not a bit like a consultant. Most of them live on a higher plane than the rest of us.' Jill sighed, but Claire bent her head, concentrating fiercely on the unappetising roast beef and what passed for a Yorkshire pudding.

'Claire?' Jill seemed to notice the strained silence, and Claire forced herself to look up.

'Do you want my custard?' she asked, trying to fend off what might have been an awkward question. 'Here you are. I'll eat the apple pie, I think, and not bother with the main. The roast beef must have come off a very elderly ox!'

'Oh, ta! Have you heard when the new woman's coming?' Jill asked, 'I suppose not.'

Oh, yes, Mr Colby's 'intimate acquaintance'. 'Yes, I've met her, actually. She seems nice,' Claire said casually.

'*Does* she? I'm glad for you, though I'm sure Mr Colby's a suitable substitute! Heavens, I'll be late — see you!' Jill left, and Claire sat there for a moment thinking about Mr Colby and Sister Pountney, before deciding she would go back early and let Sister have a proper break. And, on the way, she would pop out into the grounds to have a word with Wendy Clark.

Wendy was nowhere to be seen when Claire emerged into the warm sunshine. Black tights and the heavyweight dress made her feel hot and bothered, and she decided instead to take a quick tour of the corridors. It would get her out of the sun, and Wendy must surely have come back in, unless she——

'Enjoying the sunshine, Staff Nurse?' a husky voice spoke from just behind her, bringing a flush to Claire's cheeks.

'Yes, thank you, sir,' she said in what she hoped was a respectful tone, then was disconcerted to hear Mr Colby chuckle.

'Are you off duty now?' he asked, swinging into step beside her. Depite her intention to return to the corridors to search, Claire found herself strolling across the walled garden towards the hospital annexe.

She shook her head, the movement partially dislodging the cap which rested uneasily on her squeaky-clean hair. At least, she thought, this time I'm clean and tidy *and* I washed my hair last night! 'No, I was looking for Wendy Clark,' she admitted, clutching at her cap, but it was the consultant who stopped it from falling off altogether.

'Haven't you another grip? Here, give it to me.' While a numb Staff Nurse Shaw waited, Mr Colby pinned the cap on more securely. Although his touch was as impersonal as if she had been one of his patients, she rather fancied that his eyes lingered upon her hair. It wasn't a crowning glory like Suzanne's, but it was a rich brown with just the faintest hint of red about it and glowed with health and vitality. Not being a vain girl, Claire considered her hair her only good feature, quite overlooking her other attributes.

Wishing he would go away and perversely annoyed when he raised a hand in farewell, Claire continued her search. But she couldn't resist turning back, just the once—in time to see Sister Pountney waving to the surgeon. Claire was too far away to hear any conversation, but near enough to see him lengthen his stride in his haste to speak to the sister.

Oh, well, good luck to them, Claire thought, hurrying now as she belatedly recalled her intention of giving Sister Whitelaw an early lunch.

'Ah, you're early!' Sister exclaimed, pushing the paperwork to one side as Claire hovered in the office doorway. 'How I hate all this,' she went on, waving a hand to indicate ward reports, the duty roster, scribbled notes from various doctors. 'Just a quick handover, Claire, then I'll be away. We've had to give Mrs Saunders's bed to a dysphagia—one of Mr O'Brien's patients,' Sister hurried on, Mr O'Brien being the other consultant with beds on Camber.

'What name?' Claire asked politely. Sister sometimes had the old-fashioned habit of referring to patients by their disorder, or as a 'case'.

'Whose name? Oh, the dysphagia case,' Sister went on, her lips twitching. 'A Mrs Hall, aged seventy-five. Quite a lively soul, but badly undernourished now. I was trying to keep that bed in case John wanted it, but never mind, it's really Mr O'Brien's. Now, what else is there?'

There were only one or two minor details to pass on, then Sister hurried off, while Claire paid a brief visit to introduce herself to Edith Hall.

As Sister had said, Mrs Hall looked undernourished, but assured Claire that she'd never had a big appetite. 'I've always been around eight stone, Nurse, and after my Albert died I didn't bother much with cooking.' She gave a little chuckle. 'We used to have some jokes about his name, you know. Get it? "Albert Hall"! Yes, we had some good times, me and Albert.' Mrs Hall stopped smiling and appeared to shrink in the bed, even though Claire could see she was a tall woman. It sounded almost as if she was giving up hope, and that wouldn't do.

'Mr O'Brien has suggested you might have a barium swallow, Mrs Hall, then we can see what's causing your difficulty in swallowing,' Claire explained, 'but nothing's been decided yet. In the meantime, we have to try to build you up. I expect it's easier for you to take thick rather than thin fluids, isn't it?'

Mrs Hall nodded. 'I can't take water, Nurse, it seems to "cut" my throat somehow. Tea's just the same. I've been able to get Complan down, and soup, that sort of thing, but I'm not really hungry for anything solid.'

The patient was on a fluid chart, and Claire checked it to see that it had been made out properly. 'You haven't had anything yet. Shall I get some egg custard sent up? Or Complan?'

'I wouldn't mind a bit of egg custard, dear,' Mrs Hall said, and Claire phoned down to the catering department from the office, before going into the small dayroom which was just along the corridor. Mrs Hall's daughter was in the WRVS canteen having a snack, as she had missed lunch, and would be back with her mother shortly, to see her settled in. Meanwhile, Claire wanted to see Wendy Clark, so she went into the small dayroom, which was just along the corridor from the office. Wendy was sitting watching the television, and Claire went over to her. 'Hello, I wondered where you'd got to,' she began, and Wendy gazed up blankly. 'Sorry, am I disturbing something special?'

'No, only the adverts, Claire. I likes some of them. Did you want me, then?'

This wasn't the Wendy Clark Claire had seen in the town. Then her hair had been newly permed; now it hung, limp and lifeless and badly in need of a wash. 'I saw you from the canteen and I went out to have a chat to you but you'd disappeared,' Claire explained, but the patient shook her head, avoiding Claire's gaze.

'No, I was in the bathroom, then I came in here, dear. You couldn't have seen me outside. What, go outside? I keep out of the sun!'

Yet Claire knew she hadn't been mistaken. It *was* Wendy she'd seen from the canteen window, but nothing would be gained by insisting. She held out a hand. 'If you're only watching the adverts, how would you like a nurse to wash your hair? We could find a few curlers—Sister's got an Aladdin's Cave of bits and pieces in the staffroom!'

Wendy hesitated, then got up, putting aside a blanket she'd had covering her knees. Despite the heat of the day she still looked cold.

Claire detailed the junior, Millie Baker, to take charge of Wendy, while she herself rummaged around in Sister Whitelaw's box, at length coming up with a bundle of curlers and a hairnet. She would have liked to attend to Wendy herself since they had a good rapport, but there was the medicine round, then patients had to be checked before visitors. And—Oh, heavens! Surely not a ward-round?

Clutching the curlers to her, Claire almost ran into the office, just in time to have the door closed in her face by Gram Collingwood. Annoyed, she opened it, to find John Colby about to sit in Sister's chair. A smile hovered about his mouth as he spied Claire. 'Ah, Staff Nurse—busy?' he asked, his eyes on the curlers.

Defensively, Claire said, 'They're for Wendy Clark sir. Nurse is washing her hair. Is there anything I can do for you, or shall I continue with the ward routine?'

'Mmm, yes, by all means continue, Staff.' John Colby waved a hand to indicate the patients. 'Oh, and I've a new admission coming in this afternoon. Here.' He tossed a new folder on to the desk. 'Fill in the bits and pieces, will you?'

'That's the ward clerk's job, Mr Colby,' Claire said firmly. 'She'll be back from Westfield shortly. We share her,' she explained. Westfield was Men's Surgical—Stella Pountney's ward. Then realisation dawned. A new admission! 'But we haven't a bed!'

Mr Colby idly drummed his fingers on the desk, and Claire was irresistibly reminded of last week when he had washed her face for her. *Was* it only last week?

Then he turned to Gram. 'Leave us for a moment, will you, Gram? I want a private word with Staff Nurse.' When the grinning registrar had left, Mr Colby said, 'Martin came back last night.'

'Oh? Does that mean the family's all there now?' Carefully Claire kept her tone neutral, but those piercing eyes missed nothing, and she could feel herself flush.

The consultant nodded. 'Hugh and Dorothy, Jessica, and now Martin. His wife may be joining them later.' He too, spoke in a neutral tone but Claire felt that he was warning her. Well he needn't!

'I've known Martin since we were children, Mr Colby, and I know he's married. In fact, he nearly *married* me,' she went on rashly. The fact that this was news to him was evident by the raised eyebrows and pursed lips.

'I'm sorry,' he said simply, while Claire's eyes sparked fire. There was a lot she wanted to say, but she held her tongue. Young staff nurses didn't tell consultants what they thought of them. Or if they did they were very soon looking elsewhere!

'Go on,' he encouraged. 'Say what's on your mind. It doesn't do to bottle up your feelings — didn't your psychiatric module teach you that?'

Surprised, she blurted out, 'I loved Martin! We went everywhere together, then. . .then I read in the paper about his wedding. I haven't seen him since,' she finished stonily, wondering whether he suspected her and Martin of having an affair. 'It isn't anyone else's business, sir!'

'Not mine, you mean — no, of course not. Believe me when I say I didn't mean to pry.' The consultant's voice was surprisingly gentle, and Claire had the urge to lay her poor weary head on his shoulder and weep. Well, more fool her! He probably had that effect on every woman he met — Sister Pountney in particular.

'An interesting variety of expressions crossed your face then, but never mind. Martin's been repaid for the hurt he caused you, I imagine. He looks the picture of misery.' Those deep-set eyes held Claire's and she couldn't look away, no mattter how she tried. Not that she tried all that hard, she admitted to herself later, as she supervised the admission of their new patient, Betty Plumpton.

Mrs Plumpton was well named, being several stone overweight, and a victim of stones in her gall-bladder.

Sometimes these could be dispersed without the need
for surgery, but Mr Colby had felt she would be better
without her gall-bladder and she, like Mrs Russell, was
listed for a cholecystectomy. The ward clerk had
prepared a folder for her, and Claire had checked to
see that it contained everything that was needed—
path. lab forms, weight chart, consent for op form and
so on. Now she gave Mrs Plumpton her bright, friendly
smile as Nurse Baker slowly unpacked the bedclothes
and made the bed ready for Mrs Plumpton to get into.

'I'm sorry your husband couldn't be here,' Claire
said, 'but he'll be along later, will he?'

Betty Plumpton, a northerner in her early fifties,
nodded without speaking. Despite the folklore that
said all plump people were happy, Mrs Plumpton
clearly wasn't, and Claire wondered whether she ought
to have mentioned the husband. He was down as next
of kin and of the same address, so she couldn't be
expected to know that all was not well with them.
Then, to their dismay, the patient burst out crying. It
was loud crying, childlike in its volume and intensity,
and the junior glanced at Claire in alarm. Evidently
the school of nursing hadn't prepared her for such an
eventuality. Well, it should have done, Claire thought
crossly as she put her arms about the woman. The bed-
curtains were already drawn, but that didn't guarantee
much in the way of privacy.

'Come along, we'll pop into Sister's office, shall we?'
Claire suggested, as the patient's sobs quietened.
'Hospital's a bit off-putting at first, but you'll soon get
used to us, you know. We aren't a bit frightening!'

Leaving the junior to remake the bed into its admission pack and to bring along the suitcase, Claire
guided Mrs Plumpton into the office. Tea was offered
but refused, so Claire handed her a few tissues then
waited while the woman got her feelings under control.

At length she looked up, meeting Claire's gaze. 'I'm
sorry, Nurse, but everything's got on top of me. I can't
stand the thought of another operation. I had a mas-
tectomy years ago, you know. Eeh, it was awful!'

Claire nodded, having already read the notes. 'But

you're still here. The op was worthwhile, wasn't it? I nursed a patient once who was dying from breast cancer. She had ignored the lump, and left it too late for the surgeon to save her,' Claire went on. 'You did absolutely right getting treatment in time, instead of hiding it and hoping it would go away.'

'Did I, Nurse? Well, that's nice to know.' Mrs Plumpton brightened noticeably, and Claire wondered whether she was so used to criticism, perhaps from her husband or family, that a little praise would go a long way indeed.

'Now you've decided that the nausea and pain from your gall-bladder's too much and you've made the decision to come in. That took courage,' Claire went on carefully. 'I expect you kept putting it off, didn't you? Always finding some excuse, I expect! We've loads of ladies who do that. They put their family first and forget that they're just as important.'

'Yes, that's just it, Nurse. Oh, should I call you Staff Nurse? Those uniforms throw me.' Mrs Plumpton peered at Claire's name-badge. 'Staff Nurse Claire Shaw. That's a pretty name—my granddaughter's a Claire as well.'

'Then call me Claire and you'll feel more at home. Now I'll run through the admission procedure with you, and when you're ready I'll introduce you to one or two of the others.'

Gay Wingrove would, Claire knew, take Mrs Plumpton under her wing, that same Gay who was still insisting that she wasn't well enough to be discharged but insisting more quietly now since John Colby had spent some time explaining the bed situation to her. In fact, the only way they had found a bed for Mrs Plumpton was by transferring someone to Men's Surgical! They could have done with Wendy's bed, of course, but Claire was glad they were keeping her for a couple of days.

A few minutes later she saw Mrs Plumpton settled into bed. In the circumstances, Sister had decided that the two cholecystectomies shouldn't be warded together. Each might feed off the anxiety of the other, and Claire could see the sense of that view. 'Annie, our house surgeon, has been bleeped, and she'll be along as soon as she's free,' Claire explained as she whisked the bed-curtains right back so that the patient could see the others in that corner of the ward. 'That lady at the end if Mrs Wright, and next to you is Mrs Wingrove. Ladies, this is Mrs Plumpton, who's come in to stay for a few days. Make her welcome!'

Leaving Nurse Baker with the new patient, Claire bustled away to get the patient-history notes from the office, then stopped as she saw Sister Pountney beckoning to her from the other end of the corridor. Wearily she retraced her steps.

'Yes, Sister? Oh, our new admission has just arrived. Is Annie on your ward?'

'She's been and gone — there's an emergency somewhere.' Sister Pountney sounded abstracted. 'Look, are you seeing Mr Colby at all? Your new admission won't need him, will she?'

Surprised, Claire shook her head. 'No, Sister, not today. Mr Colby should be in Outpatients now.'

'Well, he isn't, and I particularly wanted to get a message to him. He lives near you, doesn't he? Could you pop a message into him on your way home?' When Claire didn't immediately answer, Stella Pountney raised a thin brow. 'Is that too difficult for you? I thought you were both living in Hemsley Green. It's only a one-horse village, isn't it?'

Claire bridled. 'I know where he's lodging. I can push a note through the letterbox if you like,' she said reluctantly. She didn't see why she should act as messenger-girl for Sister Pountney and, more importantly, she didn't want to visit Hemsley Manor. She might see Martin and she wasn't ready.

'I'll put it in an envelope and you can come and fetch it before you go off duty.' Without a word of thanks, the slightly built sister went back to her ward, leaving Claire feeling less than charitable. It would be interesting to see Mr Colby again, off duty. On the other hand. . . On the other hand, Claire decided she would rather not.

It seemed strange to her that the charismatic Colby should be interested in Stella Pountney, who had nothing going for her that Claire could see. She was attractive in an ice-maidenish sort of way and had a lovely figure, Claire acknowledged, trying to be fair, but there was nothing special about her, and surely there was a Mrs Colby somewhere?

Perhaps the mysterious Mrs Colby would appear at the manor. And, with any luck, Martin Medhurst would not.

CHAPTER FOUR

ONLY Dandy saw Claire drop Sister Pountney's note through the letterbox at the manor. Pausing just a moment to gaze up at the gaunt grey flint building, Claire felt a pang of what might have been homesickness. She had spent much of her childhood there, after all. One day the manor would belong to Martin and his wife, assuming they were still together. But one day it might have been mine, Claire couldn't help thinking. Mine and Martin's, our children's and *their* children's. . .

At last she turned away, Dandy's shrill yapping and whining breaking into her reverie. She couldn't resist going over to where the dog's snout was pressed up against the fine mesh netting which had been placed along the lower railings by the side-gate. 'Sorry, old friend, I've got to go,' Claire crooned, reaching her hand over the netting to stroke his head and pull his ear. 'See you some time!'

This time she hadn't cycled, she had come in her car straight from the hospital, and she was almost ready to pull away from the carriage circle when a man came running up from the direction of the summerhouse — their summerhouse in the old days. It was Martin!

Claire gave him a cool wave, then set the car in motion, accelerating smoothly away. She could see him gesturing to her, but no way was she going to stop. It hurt, but she had to keep going. She saw now that Martin belonged in the past. If he and his wife intended to divorce, that would be different, but if it was merely a trial separation then Claire felt she couldn't try to widen the gap between them. She simply wasn't made that way, and couldn't take her happiness at the cost of someone else's misery.

Finding that tears were rolling down her cheeks, she angrily dashed them away, then spent the rest of the short journey trying to divert her own attention by wondering what was in Stella Pountney's sealed and scented envelope!

Since Suzanne lived and worked in London during the week, Claire was alone in the house for much of the time, and once she was home she wandered out to the patio, her sombre thoughts weighing her down. What, she wondered, had Martin been going to say? Did he want to renew their relationship?

Speculation was idle and completely fruitless, she decided, eyeing the jungle grimly. Tired though she was, she was going to mow the lawn and give Suzanne the surprise of her life when she returned on Friday evening. That, however, would have to be after she had tidied the house a bit. Suzanne was an excellent organiser and her party last evening had gone with a swing, but she was less enthusiastic about clearing up afterwards. In fact, she had insisted on leaving everything until this morning, probably in the faint hope that their once-weekly help would tidy up, and Claire eyed the living-room gloomily. This was where the ravages of the night really showed. Worse than the crumpled cushions, records and CDs everywhere was the faint smell of cigarette and cigar smoke.

Well, set to work, Staff Nurse Shaw, set to work! 'Setting to work' yielded some surprising results. Claire gathered the rubbish together in one corner then surveyed the unexpected items she'd picked up: a pair of snazzy silk stockings, a pretty brooch, and a wallet belonging to one of Suzanne's men friends which yielded a sum of money and five credit cards!

After she had left a message on the Ansaphone at Suzanne's swish London pad, Claire belatedly wondered to whom the silk stockings belonged, but had thought it better not to mention them. Suzanne might——

'Busy, Staff Nurse?' a familiar voice enquired, and Claire turned towards the open window, the stockings clutched in one hand. John Colby's gaze dropped to them for a moment. 'Very sexy—where are the scarlet garters?'

Claire chuckled. 'That would be telling! I found them when I was clearing up. Would you like some lemonade? Or an ice-cream?' she offered, wondering why he had come. Had he too seen her at the manor and thought she was running after Martin? Well, he could mind his own business!

'Will there be arsenic in the lemonade and warfarin in the ice-cream, Nurse—or are you planning a more sophisticated punishment? A vat of malmsey, perhaps?'

Claire flushed, the more so when the surgeon began to laugh. 'Well, I wasn't!' she said enigmatically. 'It's a bit fusty in here. I'll bring the lemonade out,' she went on, indicating the patio where yesterday's chairs and loungers were still waiting invitingly.

'I could do with a little sun-lounging,' he admitted, and when Claire appeared at the French windows with a tray of cool drinks it was to find her uninvited guest making himself comfortable on Suzanne's sun-lounger.

He glanced up at her from under black lashes as she approached, then rose to take the tray from her. Claire was careful to see that their fingers didn't touch, and the slight smile on his face was evidence that he had noticed. 'I found a few biscuits in case you're peckish,' she announced. 'We had a party last night and there isn't much left.'

His eyebrows shot up. 'We?' he probed, accepting the glass of lemonade Claire poured for him. 'You live with someone?'

'I don't live alone,' she said primly. 'There's too much house for one person,' she added.

'Too much garden as well, I should say. The Medhursts' gardener and his son have left the area so they're looking about for a replacement. Who does yours?' he wanted to know, and Claire pointed to herself. 'On your own? Doesn't this person you live with help out?' Claire saw the spark of amusement in his eyes.

'No, I do most of it myself. Well, no, that isn't really true,' she conceded. 'We sometimes have a gardener but we're between them at the moment. They don't

stay very long.' That was no lie. Even jobbing garden-
ers wouldn't stay once Suzanne started interfering with
their work. She had a habit of leaving them long lists
of things she wanted altered. Then there was the
episode of the Grecian statues. . .

Claire's mouth curved into a smile. The four-foot
tall statues had been a particularly short-lived idea,
and once Suzanne had lost interest it had fallen to
Claire to dispose of them.

'Let me in on the joke, won't you?' The surgeon's
voice was amused, indulgent, and Claire glanced at
him in surprise.

'I was thinking about the statues. We decided to
have one or two in the garden but it didn't work out
and I gave them away. They represented the muses,
mainly — you've probably seen them in the manor
gardens.' Perhaps, even now, Martin was taking tea in
the rose-garden beside one of them, possibly Erato,
the muse of love poetry! Resisting the urge to giggle,
she went on, 'Did you get Sister Pountney's note? She
couldn't find you in Outpatients so she asked me to
pop a note through Mart — through the Medhursts'
letterbox.'

'Through Martin's letterbox. Yes, I was behind him
as you drove away like one of the furies, rather than a
muse. *That* particular statue is down by the lake,
incidentally. What on earth possessed you to waste
money on them?'

Not wanting to mention Suzanne and her short-lived
enthusiasms, Claire merely smiled, then drained her
glass of lemonade and got up. 'Sorry I can't stop to
talk, Mr Colby, but I have to —— '

'Call me John when we're off duty. Your delightful
Sister Whitelaw does.' He chuckled, and Claire's lips
twitched, she could well imagine Sister making a pet
of him.

'I've decided to mow the lawn now, so you'll have
to excuse me,' she said firmly, picking up the tray and
carrying it back into the house. He followed her,
though, and stood leaning against the partition which
divided the kitchen and dining area. It was a big room,

but now it seemed to Claire's eyes that it had shrunk. Although a tall man, the surgeon certainly didn't block out the light, but there didn't seem enough space for them both, somehow. Feeling suddenly clumsy, she almost dropped the glass jug but managed to catch it in time, before setting it to one side while she rinsed out the glasses. All the while she was conscious of John's eyes watching her, and she could feel her cheeks growing heated. Why on earth didn't he say something?

When at length he did, Claire rather wished he had remained silent. 'Martin was coming over this evening, but I said if he had any messages for you I would pass them on.' His voice was expressionless, but Claire whirled round. How dared he?

'Thank you *very* much, Mr Colby! If Martin wants to see me, why shouldn't he? Unlike you and Stella Pountney, we don't need a message-carrier!' Belatedly aware that she was being insolent to someone who could, if he wished, make life intolerable for her at the hospital, Claire stopped and nibbled her lip.

'Think first, Staff Nurse, *then* speak.' Thankfully, John seemed to find her remark amusing, but that made her cross, too. He didn't take her seriously!

Realising she was being perverse, Claire tried to mend matters. 'I'm sorry, but Martin and I might have things to say to each other. Even if it's only to reminisce about our childhood,' she said, unaware how wistful she sounded.

John seemed about to comment, then closed his mouth again, that rather hard expression reappearing in his eyes, just as it had on the ward first thing that morning. He still looked tired, but Claire knew better than to comment on it.

'I expect you want to get home now,' she said instead, and he shot her quizzical look.

'Getting my marching orders, am I? You're right, I have things to do at the manor, but if you lend me some gloves I'll have a go at the lawn for you,' he offered, and Claire's mouth opened in astonishment. A consultant offering to mow the lawn!

'I think the last gardener left some old ones. I'll have a look, but there's no need, really,' she assured him. 'I'll do it tomorrow. We——'

'Whoever this "we" is, I shall be long gone before he returns from work, don't worry.' He sounded grim, and Claire was about to explain about Suzanne, then changed her mind.

The shrilling of the telephone broke into the strained silence, and John reached it before her. Claire heard Suzanne's honeyed tones, and sighed. Here we go again, she thought, then wandered into the living-room. But she could hear the consultant's muted laughter even from there. Darn Suzanne! Why couldn't she ring *after* John Colby had gone about his business? The receiver was replaced, and Claire had schooled her face into its usual cherubic innocence when John appeared in the doorway.

'That was the "he" you live with, or so I gather! Suzanne demanded to know why she was speaking to a man instead of to her little cousin, and asked me to tell you to behave yourself!'

He was grinning now, and Claire had to struggle to keep her voice steady as she said, 'I'll bear that in mind. I suppose she's coming home in the week?' Suzanne would, she knew, wish to investigate!

'She didn't say—merely thanked you for the message and asked you to keep the wallet and credit cards safe until she can pick them up. Her friend was frantic with worry when he found he'd lost them. She doesn't know who owns the brooch, but she'll make enquiries. Were all the guests people from London?' John asked, and when Claire nodded he went on, 'None of your own friends?'

Claire pushed back that lock of hair that wouldn't be tamed. 'No—my friends are all at the hospital. Suzanne's friends are all trendy advertising people.'

'I see. Well, what about those gloves, young Claire?' They traded glances. Claire didn't care to be called 'young Claire' in that manner. He wouldn't call her cousin 'young Suzanne', that was for sure!

'Is Suzanne glamorous? She sounded it,' he commented, and Claire was certain he had read the uncharitable thoughts in her mind.

'Very,' she said succinctly. 'I'll get the gloves, but. . .' She hesitated. 'Should you be doing manual work? What about your nice clean hands?'

'I'll take good care of my hands, don't worry. Mowing won't hurt them — but thank you for your concern,' he added, an inscrutable expression on his face.

To Claire's dismay, the owner of the nice clean hands decided to expose some other part of his anatomy to the sun, and he had whipped off his casual checked shirt by the time she returned with the gloves. She wouldn't have been human if she hadn't felt a *frisson* of awareness as she glanced at that magnificent male torso, and, cross with herself, she turned away once she had presented him with the mower.

As Claire finished tidying, she could hear the roar of the mower as her boss got busy with his self-imposed task. It was a comforting sound, and she felt almost happy, content. It was an odd feeling — Martin had never made her feel like that.

Ah, Martin! She sank down on to the settee. John was out of sight now and she looked inward instead, at Martin. With him life had been exciting. Traumatic, too, she acknowledged, trying to be honest. Being left dangling, never knowing when or if Martin was going to ring — *that* hadn't been exciting. By then she had moved into the nurses' home as it hadn't seemed right to take advantage of the Medhursts' hospitality any longer. Then Suzanne had returned, given Claire her blunt — and unflattering — opinion of Martin, then urged her to share the house she was thinking of buying in Hemsley Green, Claire's own home having been sold to the new practice.

The glamorous, globe-trotting Suzanne had suffered a disappointment in love, or, as she herself put it, 'He forgot to tell me he already had a wife', so buying the house between them and sharing expenses had been the best thing to happen to Claire in a long time. Then Suzanne had become bored with Hemsley Green and decided to live up in London during the week. Claire foresaw a time when her cousin would stay there permanently, then they would have to let the house go. Back to the nurses' home, she supposed, not disliking the idea. And Martin? No, he didn't figure in her own future plans at all. Martin was in the past.

Confident that even meeting Martin again would have no visible effect on her, Claire had laid ice-cream and wafers on the patio table by the time one locum consultant surgeon had finished doing the gardener's work.

'Thanks for doing the lawns, John. How about some ice-cream?' Claire indicated the table, and the surgeon grinned before taking off his gloves and mopping his sweaty brow with the towel she handed him.

'Sounds good, looks good, and, by heaven, it *is* good!' he quipped, smiling down at her. 'Though a cool beer would be equally welcome,' he added, and Claire pulled a face.

'No such luck. Suzanne's the only one who drinks and — Oh, there might be some left from the party.' Claire doubted it, her cousin's friends being of the hard-drinking variety, but she could look, anyway.

The cocktail cabinet having yielded only half a bottle of Advocaat and a little brandy, Claire went in search of John, who seemed to have vanished. Then she heard voices the second before he reappeared around the side of the house, by the roses. He was talking to Martin Medhurst!

Claire felt faint. Despite her confidence in her heart's powers of recovery and her certainty that Martin's attraction was all in the past, she now found to her dismay that she had been wrong: sight of him still affected her, still sent her pulses racing and her heart beating in an alarming and erratic fashion. No, the attraction wasn't dead and buried — far from it!

Yet none of these unsettling thoughts showed on her face as she smiled a welcome to the man she would, once, have followed to the ends of the earth. 'Welcome back, Martin! I heard on the grapevine that you're all at home again.'

Martin's smile was as warm as ever, but Claire saw the lines of strain around his eyes and mouth, the flabbiness of his once trim physique. His wife had let him go to seed! Typically Claire didn't blame the man himself, but if she had been his wife she would have seen he followed a sensible diet, took regular exercise, and. . . Just in time Claire pushed her nursing self to one side. Who was she to arrange anyone's lifestyle?

He took her hand, to Claire's embarrassment, aware as she was of a certain darkly brooding presence in the background. Not that it was any business of John's, she thought resentfully, urging Martin to join them. 'I'll get another bowl of ice-cream. Or would you prefer a soft drink?'

Her loved one patted his midriff, or 'spare tyre' as it might uncharitably have been called, then shook his head. 'No, thanks, Claire — got to watch my weight. Father lost nearly two stone in Spain and it makes me feel a bit porky, I can tell you! I'll just sit and enjoy the view. Quite like old times, eh?'

Claire returned his smile, not sure she wanted reminding about old times. Memory of some of their old times, indeed, she had suppressed. Aware that she was blushing, Claire sat between the two men, who conversed easily together, mainly about travel. Nor was she forgotten, for John took every opportunity to bring her into the conversation, though Claire had to admit she hadn't done much globe-trotting.

'Father wants to be off on his travels again,' Martin put in. 'It was Mother who pined for Hemsley Green, would you believe it?'

Claire badly wanted to ask how long the family would remain at the manor — or, rather, how long Martin would remain there — but felt constrained by John's presence. The more so when her gaze accidentally met his, and she saw the smile hovering about his mouth. Darn the man!

Then he glanced at his watch, frowning. 'Is that the time? I promised Dandy a run later, and I've got some papers to key in. I'll see you back at the house, Martin!'

With a friendly smile for Claire and a long, considering look for Martin, the surgeon shrugged into his discarded shirt then walked briskly away, Claire's eyes following his tall, lean figure. Well, at least he'd had the grace to give her a few moments alone with Martin, but she was suddenly wary, not knowing what to say, how to behave. Some vital essence had disappeared from the garden, or perhaps it was because the sun had gone behind a hitherto unnoticed cloud. Whatever it was, Claire shivered, then moved away, not wanting Martin to think she was hoping for an embrace to warm her.

'It's been a long time, Claire.' His voice was calm, cool, not a bit lover-like, and she whirled around. Martin was standing with his arms folded, watching her.

Claire found her voice and summoned up a small smile. 'Yes, it has. Is everything all right? Your job, I mean,' she hurried on, not wanting to hear about his marriage, but to her dismay that was what she did hear about.

'Oh, Claire! It hasn't worked out, but I still love Jacinth, you know.' Martin's voice was morose as he wandered over to where Claire stood as if turned to stone. He rested a hand lightly on her shoulder and she closed her eyes, willing herself not to react to his touch. 'I've missed you, my pet. I can always talk to you. You always understood me — Jacinth doesn't,' he finished, his voice full of bitterness.

Claire remained silent, her mind numb. He still loves his wife. 'You always understood me'. That was it. She understood him too well — understood that he had never loved her. She had simply been Claire, the girl he had been brought up with. Yet he *had* spoken words of love, even though he seemed to have forgotten. He had done more than that, she reflected sadly. She and Martin had become lovers. She had been good enough for *that*, even though the thought of actually marrying her had apparently never entered his head. She pushed back a tendril of hair. Yet she'd been so sure, so certain that it was only a matter of time before

they would be man and wife! She wouldn't have. . .
Not if she had realised. . . She wasn't that kind of girl.
Old-fashioned, Suzanne had once called her, then
given her a hug and told her it was the best way to be.

How little you know, Suzanne. Claire almost spoke
the words aloud, but, even if she had, Martin wouldn't
have heard, for he was still speaking as if unaware of
her stunned silence.

Mentally shrugging, she pinned her professional
smile to her face. Later, she would cry for her crushed
dreams, but for now she would let Martin talk. He
would undoubtedly feel better afterwards — but Staff
Nurse Shaw most certainly would not.

CHAPTER FIVE

IT WAS a relief to go on duty the following morning, even though it meant the start of a very long day. After her sleepless night, Claire felt drained of all emotion, but no one seemed to notice anything amiss as she took the handover.

'Mrs Russell's been prepped, ready for Theatre,' Bibi told her. 'She's first down. Mr Colby rang to put a "hold" on Mrs Plumpton but he didn't say why. Both of them had a good night, as far as we could tell. But every time we checked, Wendy Clark was sitting up and staring into space,' Bibi commented. 'She told me she doesn't want to go home but I couldn't get any more from her. I think she's lonely at home, you know.'

Claire agreed. 'At least here she has the other ladies, though she's never been much of a mixer. I wonder if it's family problems again?' she mused, recalling that Wendy's grown-up children were as prickly and huffy a bunch of people as any she'd met. 'Still, I'm on a split duty so I'll have a chat to her after ops,' she confirmed.

'Rather you than me. God, a whole day in this place! Good old night duty — see you, Claire!' Bibi took herself off, leaving Claire wondering if a change to night shift might be a good thing. Then, recalling herself, she quickly sorted out the duty roster. Thank goodness it was an operating day and would fly by, so that she wouldn't have time to think about Martin and the shattering knowledge that he hadn't spent the last three years pining for her!

Bad for your ego, Staff Nurse, but you'll survive, she told herself, before shrugging Martin — and her own problems — aside. There was no time for introspection on an ops day. Most of their beds were John Colby's and it was his list this morning. Claire smiled slightly. Every time she saw him now she would mentally strip away the neat suit or white coat, leaving him bare-chested — *that* was a highly improper thought and one she must suppress!

Nursing duties allocated, Claire went round the ward saying good morning to the patients. Dora Russell was dozing behind screens and Claire detailed the second-year, Nurse Swaffield, for theatre duties. This involved accompanying the patient to the theatre ante-room, handing over documentation and any other relevant information, and was also an opportunity to reassure the patient on the way. Mrs Russell would need plenty of that, despite Claire's talk with her yesterday.

But why, Claire wondered, had John said not to give Betty Plumpton her pre-med? And was she to have a light breakfast, perhaps being rescheduled for the afternoon? Leaving them all wondering like this, and, more importantly leaving the patient to worry herself into such a state that her BP would shoot up, was totally unacceptable behaviour on the part of the surgeon.

Her hand hovered over the telephone once she was back in the office. She had left out those patients in Mrs Plumpton's cubicle, since she could hardly answer any questions until she knew the answers herself. Well, John Colby had better have a few answers when she rang down!

As if her imagination had conjured him up, there was his tall figure, in jeans and T-shirt, his gaze thoughtful as it rested upon her, and Claire could feel her own BP rising.

'I was just about to ring down, sir,' she said crisply. 'What about —— ?'

'Mrs Plumpton,' he finished for her. 'Mr Plumpton's run off with another woman, and I'm not sure what to say to her.' The surgeon ran long, blunt fingers through his damp, tousled hair.

'Oh!' Claire said, her own little worries seeming even smaller now. 'The poor soul! I wondered why he hadn't been in to see her. But she must have known

about it, surely?' Her questioning eyes were turned
towards the surgeon, seeking reassurance. Seeking
comfort, too, she realised. Yet again she felt safe,
cared for, in the presence of John Colby.

'Who knows? She hasn't mentioned him to you at
all?' At Claire's quick shake of the head, John went
on, 'Probably deep down she knew it was only a matter
of time, but to leave her *now!* It's indefensible. A
patient must be psychologically prepared for surgery,
not just physically,' he went on, almost to himself.
'Does she suspect, and would it be harmful to operate
in these circumstances?'

'It took a lot of courage for her even to come in,'
Claire ventured, 'but she's a plucky lady, from what
I've seen of her. How did you come to hear about Mr
Plumpton? Was it her social worker?'

'Yes, they've apparently been rallying around, but
it was a pity they couldn't have persuaded the man to
hang on for a while, just until his wife was over her
op. I don't like operating on such an obese woman,
anyway.' John paused, his eyes bleak. 'I hate to be less
than open with a patient but I don't think I'll tell her,
Claire. Does she have visitors at all? Anyone who
might have carried the news.'

Claire reached for the visitors' book. 'Sister likes a
record kept of visitors. This way she can keep a check
on relatives who never come, or anyone who upsets
the patients,' she explained. 'I wasn't on yesterday
evening but — yes, here we are.' She turned the book
so that they surgeon could see for himself. To do this,
he had to move nearer the desk and this was too close
for Claire's comfort. A fresh, tangy smell of aftershave
wafted down to her as he bent his dark head.

'Mrs Skelton,' he read out. 'Any relation to Mrs
Plumpton?'

'It doesn't say she is, but the part-timers might not
have asked. I'll check with Nurse Wise — she's the
mature student. She's also Mrs Plumpton's named
nurse, so they've been building up a relationship,'
Claire went on. A named nurse was the person
delegated to a particular patient, someone to whom

the patient could relate and who would deal with any questions, or attempt to sort out any problems that arose for that particular patient. Although the scheme had its drawbacks, Claire felt it gave them confidence knowing that there was a special nurse for whom they might ask.

'Oh — what about the pre-med? If I go near Mrs Plumpton, she'll ask about that. If she's second she ought to have it soon,' Claire said.

'Leave it for now. I'll take her later — just find out about the visitor, will you? Then I'll have to get down myself.'

As luck would have it, Natalie Wise was talking to Mrs Plumpton, so Claire had no option but to go up to the bed. It looked dramatic to beckon or call the student, and it wouldn't take much for Mrs Plumpton to get suspicious. 'Pop into the office, will you, Nurse? Mr Colby wants a quick word before he goes to Theatre. Something about a surgical project,' Claire said hastily, aware of the patient's anxious expression.

'Is everything all right, Mrs Plumpton? We'll be coming to give you your pre-op medication shortly but we've had to rearrange the operating list,' Claire went on brightly. That was no less than the truth, and the reason for it need never be known.

'As long as it's this morning, dear,' Mrs Plumpton said wearily. Then came the question Claire had dreaded. 'I suppose you haven't heard anything from Wally? That's my better half, if you can call him a "better" half. I thought he might have phoned.' Mrs Plumton's voice was bitter, and Claire's eyes darkened with sympathy.

She didn't quite know what to say. If she said John had heard, she would be flying in the face of his instructions not to tell the woman, and that might prove to be a fatal setback for her. On the other hand, she thought, never lie to patients, for that way you destroyed their confidence in you. Well, she certainly wasn't about to do that. 'I haven't heard from him, but perhaps Mr Colby has. Is he meant to be coming in later?' Claire said after a momentary pause.

Their eyes met, and Mrs Plumpton merely nodded, before glancing down at her hands which were clenched on the sheet. Claire put her arm around her. 'I've left Mr Colby in the office but I'll be back presently — and I'm on duty this evening as well so we can have a bit of a chat then,' Claire promised, reluctant to leave but knowing the consultant must be faced.

Natalie Wise was still in the office, and to Claire's astonishment she and the consultant were discussing computers! Face flushed, the nurse turned at Claire's entrance. 'Sorry, Staff,' she murmured, before hurrying out, leaving Claire to ask blandly, 'Did Nurse know who Mrs Skelton was?' John's eyes narrowed — almost as if he knows I didn't succeed in putting Mrs Plumpton off the scent, she thought resentfully. He didn't *need* a computer!

'A neighbour, she thinks. Certainly not a close relative, anyway, and she apparently didn't say anything about her husband. Mrs Plumpton doesn't suspect?' His voice was sharp, and Claire hesitated then admitted she probably did.

'But I didn't tell her!' Claire felt bound to defend herself, though she doubted that she would be believed. 'She asked if I'd heard from Wally and I said I hadn't. Which is true,' she added quickly. 'I said perhaps you had, but she just gave me a look and then. . . Yes, I'm sure she knows,' Claire had to concede, and the surgeon gave an exasperated sigh.

'You had no business mentioning him! But never mind, the damage is done,' he went on before Claire could put him right. 'I'll have to speak to her now, I suppose. One might have thought you would have put the patient's needs before this urge to tell the truth no mattter what it costs!'

That was too much, and Claire opened her mouth to give him a piece of her mind, but, perhaps fortunately, Sister Whitelaw appeared and the opportunity was lost. Leaving her senior to deal with one irritating consultant, Claire escaped.

When at length she had time on her hands, she

found that John had given instructions for Mrs Plumpton to be discharged. Aghast, Claire could only stare at Sister, who delivered this information with an unsmiling face. 'He says he can't operate on her now, Claire, not with this hanging over her. Wouldn't be right.'

'Oh! She does know about her husband, then?' Claire faltered. 'Mr Colby blames me, but she guessed, Sister! Shall I help her pack?'

'No, let Nurse Wise do it. Always better to let the named nurse help them — and don't blame yourself, Claire. Mrs Plumpton stood up for you — said she'd guessed all along how it would be. But now it's come, she's shaken up, and keeps saying if she hadn't agreed to the operation she'd have been at home to persuade him to stay. If my husband were that sort, I'd help the bugger to pack!' Sister went on, with a touch of her usual dry humour.

Claire tried to laugh, but to her horror she found tears in her eyes instead. 'I'll get on, then,' she murmured, turning away. Poor Mrs Plumpton — having plucked up her courage to have the operation, then to have it cancelled because she was judged unfit for surgery. And all because of a man! Men were the very limit and ought to be banned.

All the Camber ops patients, bar one, had returned from the recovery-room by the end of the morning shift. They remained there until they were fully conscious, since Recovery had a better nurse-patient ratio than any ward could afford. Camber was no exception, Claire reflected as she went to make a final check of the post-op patients while one of the part-time staff nurses supervised the rest of the ward. She herelf would stay on until Sister returned from first lunch, then have four hours off before returning to Camber for the evening, since there was no one else to take charge. Already her back ached and her feet hurt, but nothing dimmed her cheerful smile as she greeted Dora Russell.

'Can you hear me, Mrs Russell? You're so quiet I

nearly forgot you!' Claire joked as she paused by the
bed, to be rewarded by a wan smile. Mrs Russell's
gall-bladder had proved difficult to dissect because of
adhesions, and the operation had taken longer than
planned. Now she was clearly exhausted and needed
more sleep. There was a tightness, too, about her
mouth that suggested pain.

'Is it really over?' she whispered, and Claire
squeezed her hand.

'Yes, it's really all over, and Mr Colby's pleased
with you. Now—are you in any discomfort? Would
you like me to get you something to make you feel
easier?'

The patient nodded. 'I'd like these odd tubes out of
my body, though. I'll feel better and look better when
they've gone. Can you take them out now?'

'I'm sorry, but you'll have to keep them for a day or
two. Do you remember my telling you before the op?'
Claire asked. 'The drain stays for two or three days,
just to drain the gall-bladder bed, and you need fluids
so that's why the infusion is running—but I'll get an
injection ready for you then you can sleep,' Claire
went on firmly, 'and we can talk again this evening. I'll
be back in a jiffy.'

After she had given the intramuscular injection,
Claire checked their other post-op patients but for
once there were no nursing problems. One patient
must have posed a dilemma for John though, she
reflected, automatically checking the pulse of Miss
Upton. She'd had a laparotomy, which was an exploratory operation, an 'opening up' to see what was inside
the abdomen if the surgeon was unsure of the diagnosis
or wanted confirmation of a diagnosis already made.
The mass John's team had found was judged inoper-
able so the incision had been closed and Miss Upton
returned to the ward, to await transfer to a more
suitable place for terminal care in due course.

A busy surgical ward was no place to die, Claire
thought bitterly, stroking back the patient's thin hair.
Although she was only in her early seventies, which
was far from old, Grace Upton was old in other ways.

A thin, almost emaciated woman apart from the distended abdomen, she lived alone and probably existed on tea and bread and butter.

Saddened, Claire was about to return to the office when Miss Upton's eyes flickered open and gave her a long, considering look. Then the patient smiled, a smile of such genuine warmth that Claire wanted to cry. Instead, she beamed down at her, then dropped a kiss on her brow. 'I'll see you at supper-time, Miss Upton. I'm off now for the afternoon. Take care.'

Knowing she took the loss of patients too personally and that she ought to harden her heart, Claire also knew she would never change. Caring was what nursing was all about. If you didn't care enough, you might as well give it all up. Her thoughts kept pace with her soft footsteps as she went off duty for her break, and it was as she began her long walk along the corridor that she saw John Colby, who was evidently also taking his break. He was standing by the lift, deep in conversation with a nurse who had third-year stripes on her cap, but it wasn't until Claire had passed, all the while trying her darnedest to be invisible, that she realised: it was Natalie Wise.

Claire heard their muted voices as she hurried along. Were they, she wondered, still discussing computers? She would have given a lot to know.

Lunchtime, unfortunately, brought a meeting with Martin, and Claire was sorry now that she'd given in to his pleading. Her lunch with him wasn't a success, and only partly because John was a witness to their meeting.

It was, Claire supposed, her own fault for suggesting that they eat in the cheap and cheerful restaurant favoured by the hospital staff as it was only a stone's throw from the hospital gates, and served meals all day. Martin had other ideas as they met outside the Horse and Crown. 'Look, why don't you fix me a bite to eat at your place? I can't say I think much of this.' He indicated the brightly painted exterior. 'Seem a weird lot of people going in.'

'That's because they're nurses, I expect.' Claire 's

voice was icy. 'I often eat here, but we can go right into town if you would rather?'

'Oh, all right—a little home cooking is just what I need, though,' Martin said grumpily. 'It's been chips with everything recently, and I need to cut down. Eat green, so to speak!'

'Yes, I thought you were running to fat,' Claire said without thinking.

'Thank you, Nurse Shaw,' Martin said with a faint smile, 'but you're right, of course. Perhaps you could put me on a diet? You know, give me a diet sheet or estimate the calories I need?'

'Oh, yes,' Claire murmured, wondering whether she was to hand out free medical advice as well. Nothing was turning out as she had planned. Certainly the old attraction was there—on her part, anyway. But this Martin Medhurst was a stranger and she wasn't sure she liked him. He was gradually slipping down from the pedestal on which she had set him since his marriage. Well, more fool her! She must be practical, learn to accept him as he was, not as she would like him to be. 'You might begin now,' she suggested. 'They do lovely salads here and you can have vanilla ice-cream for pudding.'

Martin shuddered, but later pronounced himself satisfied with the large mixed salad Claire had ordered. 'I could do with a stiff whisky, though,' he went on morosely, but Claire shook her head, trying to keep a smile fixed to her face. It wasn't easy, particularly when your heart was breaking.

'You'll have to cut down on alcohol, Martin. It's the only way,' she told him. 'I think——' But Martin was never to hear what Claire thought, for at that moment she met the unsmiling gaze of John Colby, who had just entered the Horse and Crown. And he would think she was carrying on with Martin behind Jacinth's back!

Why that should worry her Claire wasn't sure, but for some reason she wanted John's good opinion, and she had lost that now. Worse still, he was coming over—with Sister Pountney!

Sister's frosty gaze rested upon Claire for a moment, who met it blandly. Then it turned upon Martin, who had risen. Stella Pountney's ice-blue eyes softened peceptibly and another pair of blue eyes, darker ones, also surveyed Claire, who moved uneasily, hating him for making her feel guilty. Just because John was carrying on behind his spouse's back, it didn't mean Martin was! The man had a nasty mind and one day she would tell him so.

'I'll see you on the ward later, Staff Nurse. We can have a session in peace and quiet as you've two part-timers on.' Without his usual smile the surgeon looked grim, forbidding, and Claire had visions of a particularly nasty evening with him. He and Sister Pountney went to another table, and Claire glanced away hastily — to meet the disapproving gaze of Martin.

'You don't fancy John, do you?' Martin sounded scandalised, and Claire's temper rose. He was a fine one to talk!

'I'm not having an affair with Mr Colby, if that was the question! Though as you're a married man now I can't see that my private life is any of your business.' Claire's voice was brisk and businesslike, and Martin reddened.

'No, you're right, I suppose. You're a big girl now — able to choose your own men. It's just that. . .' He hesitated, then that old familiar smile appeared, and Claire's eyes widened, wondering what he was going to say. 'I don't want you to make the same mistake twice, that's all.' He covered her hand with his own for a moment. 'Good lord! Is that the time?' he muttered, making an elaborate show of glancing at the clock. 'I'd better get back — promised Father I'd go around the grounds with him, assess the damage those tenants caused.'

Claire picked up her shoulder-bag. She was glad the old Martin hadn't disappeared completely. 'I saw the hole in the hedge when I —' She stopped, but Martin seemed preoccupied and didn't press her to continue. This was just as well as she didn't want to tell him she had cycled up to the manor in the hope of meeting him!

She was back on the ward half an hour early, but even so John arrived before her. She found him sitting on the settee in the dayroom, a briefcase open in front of him. He was obviously weary after his busy operating session, but this showed only in the lines of strain about his eyes and mouth. Although he now wore his consultant's suit of dark grey, he had removed the jacket, and his silver-grey tie was askew.

He glanced up as Claire approached. 'You're early — come and sit with me.' He indicated the settee, but Claire chose instead to sit in the easy-chair.

'Are we going to talk to Wendy?' she asked, her nerves on edge in case he mentioned Martin.

'Yes, later. I've been going through her case papers. I came back late yesterday to sift them thoroughly,' John went on, surprising her.

'Do you think there's something else wrong with her?' Claire hesitated, then rushed on, 'Just because she's had a mental illness, people seem to think anything she complains of must be psychosomatic. I thought that at first,' she admitted, 'but she's looking her age now and I'm sure it isn't all mental.' Her huge, expressive eyes rested upon him in mute appeal. If there was something seriously wrong with Wendy, she was sure this man would find it.

'You really care about her, don't you?' John's eyes were kind, and once again Claire had the urge to lay her head on his shoulder and let him soothe away all her fears, all her problems. Instead, she kept her face expressionless, or so she hoped.

'I care about all our patients, but yes, Wendy is special,' she acknowledged. 'She's been investigated before and all they've found is constipation, but I think there's more to it than that,' she went on slowly.

'We ought to do some more tests, I think, though what to us are routine procedures are often uncomfortable and tiring to the patient,' he observed. 'We have to draw up ground-rules: take into account the patient's age, physical and mental condition, prospects

for several more years of useful and pain-free life,
before we subject her to further indignities. And, in
the NHS, we have to make the best use of scarce
resources, and that isn't always in the patient's best
interest.'

Claire's eyes followed him as he put the briefcase to
one side then wandered over to the window, his back
to her. 'What sort of home-life has she got? The notes
mention a married daughter living near.'

'She's got three daughters and two sons. That particular daughter used to keep an eye on her mother
but a few words were said and she doesn't go near
Wendy any more. She's rather a huffy woman,' Claire
said crossly. 'Wouldn't you think she'd swallow her
pride and rally round her mother?'

'You're an idealist, Claire! People aren't saints. See
if you can persuade Wendy to contact her — she may
not realise how ill her mother looks. Anyway, I think
we'll discharge her home for a few days, see what sort
of symptoms she gets there. Will you escort her?' The
surgeon swung round, catching Claire unawares.

Their eyes met in a moment of shared sympathy for
a patient. 'Of course, if Sister gives me permission.
We need Wendy's bed anyway.' Claire hesitated for a
moment, then plunged on, 'I'm sorry about Mrs
Plumpton, but I really didn't mention her husband.
She must have suspected all along.'

'The philandering husband — yes, I expect she did,
and I'm sorry I blamed you.' The apology was unexpected but none the less welcome, and Claire beamed

She was rewarded by a low chuckle. 'We're friends
again, are we? What were you doing with Martin?'

Claire stopped beaming. 'We were having lunch, Mr
Colby. He wanted to talk to me,' she hedged, being
unwilling to admit that Martin had spent the time
talking about his wife. It hurt that he no longer cared
even a little, but her pride wouldn't let her admit that
to anyone.

'I see.' With a sudden movement, John picked up
his briefcase, snapped it shut, then moved nearer. He
looked desperately tired. 'I know I sound like an

uncle, but don't get involved, Claire. You're too sensible to throw yourself away on a married man, I'm sure, but let the past die. OK?'

His smile was tinged with sadness and that took the sting out of his words, but even so Claire resented what he said. *He* certainly shouldn't be lecturing anyone! Mrs Colby wouldn't like to know he had been seen in a nightclub with a ward sister. Though perhaps she didn't care, Claire acknowledged. It might be one of those open-ended marriages she'd read about somewhere. She frowned, trying unsuccessfully to look severe, and John chuckled.

'You're irresistible when you're cross! Martin was a fool to throw you over.'

'He's changed and so have I,' Claire said quietly. 'I'd better get on. Staff Nurse Bignall will be —'

'Yes, that's another thing. There are far too many part-timers on this ward. Once Sister goes there won't be anyone the patients can relate to, except yourself. And what happens when you're off duty?'

Taken aback, Claire could only stare. 'Surely they'll replace Sister Whitelaw?'

The surgeon's words echoed her own thoughts. 'How can you replace a woman like that? She's held this ward together, Claire. I know they're advertising, but there will be a gap between Sister retiring and the new one starting. They save money that way,' John said grimly. 'Had you thought about applying?'

Claire admitted that she had. 'But I haven't had quite enough experience, and Sister Whitelaw will be a hard act to follow! She's special. We really need an older sister, someone motherly.'

'Possibly. I shall be sitting in judgement on the applicants so I'll see what I can arrange for you. Staff Nurse Claire wants a motherly ward sister!'

Claire raised her eyes to his. 'Sister's certainly been motherly to me, particularly when I first came to Camber. I don't know what I would have done without her.'

'You lost your mother when you were young? Is that how you came to be living with the Medhursts?'

'Mmm, that's right. Mum had a heart condition. She shouldn't have had children but she so wanted one. . . She died when I was eight and I was nearly fourteen when Dad was killed going to help an RTA, so the Medhursts took me in. Suzanne — that's my cousin — was working in Italy at the time. She's been like a sister to me as well. I may have no family of my own but people seem keen to adopt me!' Claire finished with a bright smile.

'You're special, Claire — that's why. Take care.' John leaned forward and kissed the tip of her nose. Then he was gone, and the door closed softly behind him, leaving a startled Claire to touch her face, then her nose. John Colby had kissed her!

True, it was probably the sort of kiss he might have given a daughter or a niece, but. . . But, Staff Nurse Shaw, it has brightened your day, no matter how much you might try to deny it! With that thought, Claire went back to her patients, the forlorn feeling vanishing as though it had never been.

John's research for his textbook consisted mainly of observing patient-nurse interaction, Claire had discovered, rather than actually asking direct questions of a patient. This must be why he was on the ward so much, watching, listening to patients, or just sitting beside them in the dayroom while they talked.

He was with Wendy, who was sitting by her bed, as Claire wheeled the medicine trolley into the ward a little later. Suppers were at six and she liked to get the medication out of the way first. Nurse Baker blushed the moment she espied the surgeon, and Claire hid a smile. She was sure, though, that the junior nurse hadn't had the tip of *her* nose kissed by a certain consultant!

'That Nurse Claire's a good 'un,' Wendy declared loudly as Claire came up to them.

'Does Nurse Claire meet your needs, Wendy? Is she helpful?' John asked with a smile, and Wendy snorted.

'Course she is! Always helping out — like that as a child, she was. Running errands for me, taking the old dog out. . .' Wendy glared at him as if daring him to criticise her favourite nurse, and Claire laughed.

'You stand up for me, Wendy! Here's your lactulose, and some squash if you want it.' Nurse Baker handed Wendy the glass and waited while she drank the oil, before picking up the glass and returning it to the trolley.

John's keen eyes hadn't missed that, and he nodded approvingly at Claire. 'Some nurses don't wait while the patient take the medication, Staff Nurse. I retrieved two Distalgesic from someone's bed yesterday.' His tone was mild but Claire knew the criticism was justified. She always watched even if they were so short of nurses that she had to do the medicine round single-handed, but some of the others were less careful.

'Criticism noted, sir,' she murmured respectfully, and John's chuckle followed her out of the cubicle.

There were two visiting periods on Camber Ward. The powers-that-be, or 'Upstairs', as they were jocularly known, had resisted the idea of open visiting since that would get in the way of the ward routine. *That* must be avoided at all costs, Claire thought crossly, as she began a round of the various cubicles to see that everything was ready for evening visitors. They were usually allowed in just before supper, in time to help with the meal if they wanted to.

And Mrs Dunster's grandson would certainly want to. Old Mrs Dunster was everybody's pet and Claire was always glad when she reached that bed. At ninety-one, she was their oldest patient but by far the most cheerful, and always ready to show off her bottle of gallstones to anyone who would show an interest!

'How are you, Mrs Dunster? All ready for visitors?' Claire asked, pausing by the bed.

'As ready as I'll ever be,' Mrs Dunster said stoutly, peering at Claire. 'That's young Claire, isn't it? I recognise your voice — my eyes aren't what they were. What's for supper?'

Since this was a routine question, Claire had the

answer ready. 'Soup for you, my love, with a slice of
bread to dunk in it.'

'Ah! Just what I like. I can't eat much because I
haven't seen my teeth for years, but what I *would* like
is a nice lamb chop,' the patient said wistfully, but
Claire shook her head.

'You have to watch your diet, Mrs Dunster. Even if
you could chew it, I don't think a fatty chop would do
you much good, though I——' She broke off as the
consultant reappeared.

'Who's that? Is that David?' Mrs Dunster
demanded, but the husky chuckle could belong to no
one other than John Colby. It was distinctive, thought
Claire, like the man himself. Even in a crowd John
would stand out. It was difficult to analyse, but he had
style. Suzanne also had style. Oh, bother Suzanne!

He lowered himself into the chair which was await-
ing David Dunster. 'No, I'm not David, I'm John. You
remember me, Mrs Dunster? I took out all those
fascinating gallstones.'

Mrs Dunster clutched at his hand and Claire left
them to it. He surely didn't want to examine the old
lady at visiting hour and probably he was simply
researching, but even so Claire dispatched the junior
staff nurse to attend to his needs—something *all* the
nurses were keen on doing!

Shortly afterwards, the first of the visitors came on
to the ward. At the head of the queue, as always, was
Mrs Dunster's grandson. A scholarly-looking man in
his thirties, he visited his grandmother every evening
after work, and Claire sometimes thought wistfully
how nice it must be to have someone like David
Dunster to take care of you. Although Mrs Dunster
lived in an old folks' home, Claire knew he looked in
on her her every weekend. He was married, Mrs
Dunster had told her, before snorting and saying he'd
married a load of rubbish, so Claire was left none the
wiser.

His smile was a trifle shy and his conversation stilted,
as though he found it difficult to talk to young women,
and Claire, used to brash housemen, found this oddly

endearing. She greeted him now with a warm smile. 'Your Gran's in good form today, Mr Dunster. She's just told me she wants a lamb chop!'

'That's Gran for you! More life in her little finger than some have in their whole bodies!' He paused, gazed down at the bouquet of carnations in his hand, then thrust them at Claire. 'These are for you, Staff. Gran says she's had enough flowers to last her till she's a hundred. You could put them in the office, if you don't want to take them home,' David hurried on, and, touched by the gesture, Claire cradled them to her. They were a pale yellow, her favourite colour.

'No, I shan't leave them here. I'll take them home with me tonight. Thank you — they're lovely!'

Unfortunately John Colby chose that moment to leave the ward, and his eyes rested first upon Claire's flushed face, then upon the flowers and lastly moved to David Dunster. He raised a brow just a fraction but it was enough to annoy Claire. She held out the bouquet.

'This is Mrs Dunster's grandson, sir. He's just brought these lovely flowers for. . .' She had been about to say 'the ward' but why should she feel she had to lie? 'For me,' she hurried on. 'Mr Colby, our new consultant,' she continued with scarcely a pause, and the two men shook hands. Then, with a final quizzical glance at her, John left, and an embarrassed Claire glanced down at the flowers, muttered her thanks again then dashed into the office with them, leaving David Dunster, she assumed, going in to see his grandmother.

But he was still outside the office when Claire emerged. 'Look, Staff Nurse, I'm sorry about the flowers. Mr Colby's obviously got an interest in you and I'd no right to —'

'An interest?' Claire echoed. 'It doesn't matter to him if anyone brings me flowers. There's no hospital rule against it!'

'No, I didn't mean it like that. Well, it's obvious, isn't it? I didn't realise he was your. . . Er — I'd better get to see Gran. She'll be shouting the place down if

I'm late.' He walked quickly away, leaving an astonished Claire to puzzle over his remark,

What was obvious? Surely he didn't think John had
a romantic interest in her? It was complete nonsense!
People got the strangest ideas.

It was some time after the last visitors had left that
Claire was able to get back to Wendy. Eight o'clock
and the last straggler had been seen off the ward. All
that remained, barring emergencies, was to finish
writing the report, see that patients who needed it had
been to the toilet or offered a commode, help those
into bed who couldn't manage themselves, and hand
out night sedation.

Wendy was prescribed some, but usually refused. 'I
get this feeling I'm a-going to be sick, Claire. Then I
keep wanting to spit,' she said glumly as Claire sat by
her bed. 'It's me bowels, I expect — like them doctors
keep telling me.'

Claire, having no other palatable explanation, was
forced to agree. 'You've always had trouble with them,
haven't you? Never mind — did Mr Colby tell you I'm
taking you home tomorrow? Sister will let me go after
lunch when we're not so busy, I expect.'

'Yes, I'd like that. Not that there's anyone at home,'
Wendy said sadly. 'My Richard don't get down very
often.'

'That's a shame, but what about your eldest daughter? Mr Colby thought she —'

'Well, she won't, 'cos I upset her. Mr Colby don't
know nothing about it.' With that, Wendy lay back
and closed her eyes, and Claire reluctantly left.

Wednesday was One of Those Days as far as Claire
as concerned. John's whole surgical firm descended on
them early to make a full round, and that, of course,
included Gram Collingwood, who chose to remon-
strate with Claire for talking to a patient when she
should have been scurrying around after the
consultant.

'Mr Colby knows where I am if he wants me,' Claire
said tightly. 'He's quite happy to go around with Staff
Nurse Bignall and she knows the patients as well as I

do. It's my job to see that the others aren't neglected,'
Claire went on. '*That's* why I was talking to Mrs
Green. She's apprehensive about being here at all,
despite the discomfort, and when she saw the hordes
descending she asked if she could discharge herself!'

'Sorry,' the registrar muttered, 'but when you're on
Stella Pountney's ward you'll have to toe the line a bit,
you know. She isn't like Sister Whitelaw.'

'What's that supposed to mean?' Claire demanded.
'I haven't been asked to help out on Westfield!
Anyway, I'm in charge till Sister ─ '

'Not help out, be transferred *to*. I'm sorry ─ I
thought you knew.'

'I'm being transferred to Westfield Ward?' Claire's
voice was cold, so was her expression, and the registrar
took one look at her face then gave a mock-shudder.

'Er ─ so I heard. Well, keep up the good work.' He
ambled away, leaving a shocked Claire. There must be
some mistake, there must be! They wouldn't do that
to her! Sister would soon put matters right.

Unfortunately her reaction wasn't what Claire
expected.

'It's true, Claire ─ the experience of another ward
will be good for you. I know you're ambitious and
you'll want to try for a sister's post before long. Learn
all you can before then because being a ward sister
isn't easy, believe me!' Sister Whitelaw peered at
Claire over the top of her spectacles.

'I know it isn't,' Claire pointed out. 'I often act up
for you, but I've *had* experience of other wards. I was
on Westfield before Sister Pountney went there.'

'You'll find Westfield changed for the better, Claire.
Stella might not be particularly well-liked,' Sister
acknowledged, 'but she runs an efficient ward and Mr
Colby always speaks highly of her.'

It was on the tip of Claire's tongue to say He would,
but she bit the words back. 'When do I go?'

'Next week, I'm afraid. I'd rather you stayed until
the new sister takes over here, but Upstairs have
suggested a complete swap-round of full-time trained
staff. It's typical that they haven't given anyone time

to protest, but it's all valuable experience, and it's only next door. You'll get along fine.'

Claire sighed. 'I'd better get back to the ward — there's a lot to do. Mrs Green isn't going to stay, you know. Shall I get Gram to have a word with her?'

'She's an acute abdomen, isn't she? Well, we can't force her but — No, leave it to John, he'll sort something out. He's full of bright ideas, isn't he?'

'So I believe,' Claire said grimly, 'though I can't think he would want his staff nurses moved around like so many chessmen! It isn't good for the patients *or* ward routine, sister.'

'That's where you're wrong, Claire. He asked for you to go to Westfield. Now, where did I put my pen?' Sister Whitelaw began to rummage in one of the drawers, while Claire just stood there as if turned to stone.

John had asked for her to go to Westfield! Why? For the valuable experience — or was there some deeper reason? Something to do with Staff Nurse Shaw's popularity with male visitors, perhaps? Claire was determined to find out and the sooner the better.

CHAPTER SIX

'IF WE could hold two sessions a week, Sister, or even one, how would that fit in with the ward routine?' John Colby smiled his charming smile at Sister Whitelaw, who melted visibly.

If John had asked permission to organise a Chippendales show on the ward, Claire reckoned Sister would have tried to oblige him, but fortunately he wanted something a little less outrageous. He was back on the subject of research for his textbook, and had asked if he might give lectures on Camber, though what he had in mind would benefit the present patients, not just those in the future.

'I particularly want to reach those patients who know little or nothing about the internal workings of their bodies, and who would like to ask questions — but can never find anyone who will answer them,' he went on, and Claire found herself nodding in agreement. Too often nurses would have liked to tell a patient something specific, but simply didn't understand the disease thoroughly enough to put it into 'patient-friendly' terms. Poor nurse-patient interaction, as the consultant said.

Sister pursed her lips. 'I agree in principle, John, but Upstairs won't like it,' she pointed out.

He grinned boyishly. 'I'll handle Upstairs, don't worry!'

'But you won't be here much longer,' Claire found herself saying, though it was the last thing she had wanted to say. How would they manage without his smile, his concern for the patients? How would *she* manage, which was more to the point. . .? She coloured fiercely, trying to turn her thoughts towards what was best for the patients, not what was best for her. She wouldn't miss him, not really. . .

There were murmurs of agreement from the others

crammed into Sister Whitelaw's office. Depite John's smile, Claire could almost see the steel underneath, the whipcord strength of the man, the iron determination. Realising she was making him sound like the contents of an ironmongers, she switched her unruly thoughts back to the matter in hand.

'I can accept the truth of that remark,' John was saying, 'but you'll find that Miss Wallace feels as I do — probably even more strongly. She might look as though a puff of wind would blow her over, but she didn't get where she is by being weak and yielding. There's iron determination behind that attractive façade!'

There was a ripple of amusement as John unconsciously echoed Claire's thoughts. He obviously cared about her, she mused, as the staff began to drift away. Perhaps if the lady surgeon *had* lost her husband, John would be an acceptable substitute in due course. They were just right for each other, just as she and Martin had once been right for each other, or so she had believed then. Claire gave a faint sigh, then turned to Sister with a smile. She rather thought the sister gave her one of her X-ray looks but might have been mistaken. 'Is there anything else you want me to do before I go?' Today she was due off at four, or had been, for it was now half-past.

Sister shook her head. 'No, but just do a final round, will you? I'll hang on till suppers, then Peg can take over. We've two part-timers on, haven't we?'

'Yes, until ten,' Claire affirmed. 'Oh — I've only two more days here, haven't I? I know I'm off Saturday.'

'You had last weekend with your holiday, so Stella thought you might like to start there on Sunday as she's off that day, then have three days off the following week. She isn't keen on nurses doing splits, so you'll be lucky there,' Sister bent her head to the ward report-book, leaving Claire to check the patients before going off to change.

She still hadn't taken John to task for suggesting she be moved, but she saw now it would be unwise, and

stupid as well. What did it matter? She would still see
him, still fancy him. . . No!

Cross with herself *and* with John Colby, Claire
hurried into her print skirt and sleeveless blouse,
peeled off her duty tights, thrust her bare feet into
sandals, then made her way thankfully out into the
warm evening. She closed her eyes for a moment,
feeling the breeze ruffling her hair, the sun caressing
her skin. Tomorrow was a late duty, thank goodness,
so she could sit in the jungle for a while after she had
done the shopping.

'Oh! It *is* Staff Nurse Shaw, isn't it?' A bemused
male voice hailed her just as she reached the staff car
park. David Dunster was locking his car in the public
car park which adjoined, and staring at her as though
he couldn't quite believe his eyes. Hardly surprising,
Claire reflected, since a nurse in mufti was a far
different creature from one enclosed in the heavy blue
dress, black tights and duty shoes which staff nurses at
the District were obliged to wear.

She treated him to a smile. Poor soul, he always
looked so serious, as though he had the cares of the
world on his shoulders. 'Hello, Mr Dunster. You're
early — Sister won't let you in a second before six, you
know!'

'No, I expect you're right. Look, can I give you a
lift somewhere? I can easiy drop you off and nip back
here.'

Claire shook her head, the bright hair bouncing and
gleaming in the sunshine. 'Thanks, but I've got my
own wheels.' She pointed to her Mini. 'I'm just off
home for a shower — we get so hot and sticky on the
ward.'

'Yes, you must do.'

There was a short silence which Claire didn't quite
know how to bridge, so she took refuge in a common-
place, 'It's a lovely evening, anyway. See you
tomorrow perhaps!' She waved, then hurried over to
her car. The staff car park was strictly divided into
Them and Us, as she had quickly discovered. 'Them'
included Upstairs, and people like John Colby, who

was leaning against his Mercedes with a thoughtful expression on his face.

'Oh, hello, John,' Claire said a trifle breathlessly. She could feel herself colour because of her secret knowledge, and that made her feel awkward and uncomfortable. So much so that she caught the heel of her sandal in a loose paving, and would have fallen against the Mercedes if strong hands hadn't reached out to save her. She clung to the surgeon for a moment, then quickly pulled herself free, her heart thudding madly.

'Take care, Claire—Sister Pountney will want you delivered in one piece,' John said, with a gleam in his eyes, and Claire bit her lip, trying to keep the words back. 'Go on,' he challenged. 'Say your piece.'

'I think it was mean of you to suggest that I leave Camber!' Claire flashed. 'I wasn't going to say anything, and I know it's good experience, but Camber needs a full-timer who knows the ward routine. Once Sister goes, there will only be the part-timers you keep on about. It isn't fair to anyone!' Face flushed, eyes sparkling, Claire faced John, who seemed as cool and calm as ever. Completely unmoved, in fact—so much so that she turned away and rushed over to her little car, which was parked discreetly in the opposite corner.

She had to hunt in her bag for the car keys, then a hand reached out and took the keys from her fumbling fingers and unlocked the door. 'I'm sorry,' she mumbled, turning to meet the surgeon's gaze. Sapphire eyes traded glances with deep blue eyes. 'It was stupid and immature of me. It's what's best for the patients that matters.'

'Oh, Claire!' The words seemed torn from him, and, before a startled Claire could say anything, John bent his head and kissed her full on the mouth. It was a demanding passionate kiss, and Claire knew she should struggle, make some pretence that she hated the very thought of his arms about her, but she did nothing of the sort. Instead, she melted against him, pressing her body along the length of his in a way that made her go scarlet with shame when she recalled it later, the more so when she felt John's body respond to the pressure of her own.

His lips moved from her sweet, full mouth to her ear, then brushed across her hair, and for a few wonderful seconds he held her close. Then he put her from him, her own shock mirrored in his eyes. Something else was mirrored there, too — desire. 'Claire, I'm sorry,' he murmured. 'It's hardly the appropriate place, but there'll never be an appropriate place for us. Take care.'

Claire's eyes followed him as he walked swiftly back to his car. Wonderingly she pressed a hand against her mouth, uncaring who saw her. Fortunately there was no one in her section of the car park but there might be nurses passing by. The District grapevine would go wild with excitement before morning, Claire thought, as she sat heavily down in the driving seat, then spent some minutes just staring straight ahead of her. Mr Dunster had been right, after all — John did have an interest in her.

But it was purely sexual, Claire decided, as she tentatively reversed out then swung away past the visitors' car park on her way to the main road. David Dunster was, she noted numbly, still standing by his car, and could not have failed to see her in the arms of the consultant surgeon.

'There'll never be an appropriate place for us'. Those words stayed with her all the way home.

She spent that night tossing restlessly in bed, reliving the scene over and over again. Did that kiss mean anything at all to John? More importantly, did it mean anything to her? Hadn't she been carrying a torch for Martin for the past three years and way beyond that? No, it simply wasn't possible for her to fall in love with another man. She had given Martin her all, including her heart, and if it were true love it couldn't be cast aside so easily. Yet John's kiss had stirred darker, deeper emotions that Claire hadn't known she possessed. His touch had set her body afire, not just her heart.

It was a confused, unhappy Claire who rose in the early hours unrested, and who spent another fruitless hour in strolling around the jungle before watching the sun rise in golden splendour from her seat on the patio.

Now she was so tired she could drop, and since she was on a late shift she had thankfully missed John's morning visit to the ward. That didn't mean nothing was happening on Camber, though, and there was plenty to occupy her throughout the afternoon. Dora Russell was making excellent progress, and, despite her initial wariness of the older patients, had begun making friends.

'Charles is so pleased with me!' she trilled to Claire once the afternoon visitors had gone. 'He says I don't look a *bit* ill! He doesn't feel the discomfort, though,' she added more quietly.

'If it's unbearable, you're written up for more analgesia,' Claire assured her. 'Don't put a brave face on it and endure pain because you don't like to complain.' Coming from another nurse, that last remark might have sounded a trifle tart, since Mrs Russell did nothing *but* complain, always over little, unimportant things. Claire tried to get the juniors to see that this was simply how the patient reacted to the stress of hospital admission, but at least her husband seemed grateful for all they had done for her. Two big boxes of chocolates in the office and flowers for the ward were ample proof of that!

Despite Claire's misgivings that Mrs Russell might decide to keep to her bed while she had the chance, she was up and about the day after her op, although she absolutely refused to look at the drain from her wound or the bottle which she was required to carry about with her. Now the drain had been shortened, she was free of naso-gastric and IV tubes, and spent her time wandering in and out of the other wards in the unit, probably comparing notes.

It was a pity Mrs Plumpton, their other gallstones patient, had been discharged without operation, but Mrs Dunster would be with them for another day, and

she and Dora Russell had struck up an unlikely friendship, which pleased Claire. Mrs Dunster was a sweetie
and all the staff would be genuinely sorry to see her
go. Her grandson was a different matter, as far as
Claire was concerned, and she had successfully
avoided him when he'd arrived for evening visiting,
punctual as usual. He had, after all, seen her in the
arms of the consultant surgeon, and might be excused
for thinking that that was what doctors and nurses did
in their off-duty!

Wendy had gone home, somewhat reluctantly, the
previous afternoon, with Claire as escort, and they had
just admitted Mrs Hossany, a friendly Mauritian lady
who took a keen interest in everything that went on,
requiring minute explanations for every procedure.
Claire showed her the chart Nurse Baker had prepared
for her. 'This is where we keep a record of your
progress, Mrs Hossany. There's a space for TPR —
that's your temperature, pulse and breathing rate or
respiration, and one for your blood-pressure. Will you
let Nurse Baker check your blood-pressure? She's
really an expert now!' Claire went on, and both patient
and student smiled.

'Yes, of course, my dear. You carry on.' Mrs
Hossany extended her arm. 'It's a bit on the high side,
you know? Tell me what you listen for. I'm a great
one for asking questions but my doctor's always too
busy!' She gave a wry smile.

'He wouldn't have minded explaining it to you, Mrs
Hossany,' Claire said, 'but basically each time the
heart beats blood passes into your arteries and
increases the pressure momentarily, then the pressure
falls until the next heart contraction. What we call
blood-pressure is the pressure exerted by the blood
upon the blood-vessel walls. When the pressure rises
it's called the systolic pressure and when it falls again
that's the diastolic, but don't worry about medical
terms,' she went on, seeing the woman's look of
puzzlement. 'What Nurse was doing was listening for
your heartbeat then inflating the cuff until the sound
disappeared. Then she let the cuff down slowly, and

when she heard a sound again she noted the level of mercury in the manometer, then went on letting it down until the sound of your heart beating became inaudible. Yes?' Claire turned to Millie Baker, who nodded.

'Yes, Staff. Then I recorded the two pressures on Mrs Hossany's chart — the first one was systolic and the second one diastolic,' she pronounced, and Claire gave her an approving smile before turning back to the patient.

'Blood-pressure rises with age, or medical condition, and so on. Anxiety can cause a rise as well so we like to have patients sitting or lying comfortably before we record the pressure,' she went on to explain. 'It's a simple procedure and nothing to worry about.'

Mrs Hossany, who was for barium meal investigations, seemed happy with what might have seemed a rather technical explanation, but a diagram would have been better, Claire decided. In fact, that was something she'd been meaning to talk to John about. Provided, of course, that she could catch him in an approachable mood!

It wasn't until she was writing the evening report that John appeared on the ward, but he certainly wasn't in an approachable mood. Grim-faced and stern, this was a different John Colby, the one Claire particularly disliked. His gaze swept over her. 'Anything you need me for, Staff? I'm on my way to Westfield.'

Was there anything she needed him for? Claire pondered that question for a moment, a sad smile crossing her face. If only. . . But she shook her head. 'Not at the moment. Is Mrs Dunster definitely for discharge tomorrow? I thought Gram said you would keep her over the weekend.'

'Can't be done — I'm sorry but I need her bed. She's in a home, isn't she? She'll be well looked after.'

'They aren't always well looked after in homes, though, are they?' Claire put in, determined not to agree with him. 'But she seems happy there. And her grandson visits her regularly, so —'

'Ah, yes, so he does.' Was there a slight edge to the surgeon's voice? Claire rather thought there was, and she put her head on one side, surveying him through half-closed lashes.

'Don't do that, Staff Nurse—I might be tempted again. Goodnight.' One unsmiling consultant surgeon left the ward, leaving a staff nurse wishing that he *had* been tempted again.

Then she bent her head over the report, pushing John Colby, Martin Medhurst, David Dunster and all other members of the male gender to the back of her mind. Nothing mattered except the patients.

Suzanne came home early on Friday afternoon, though Claire wasn't surprised. With an attractive man in the neighbourhood, it was as natural as breathing for Suzanne to investigate. Claire did try, though, to put her cousin off the scent.

'Being a consultant he's certain to be married,' she said as they lingered over their evening meal. It was a Chinese take-away which Suzanne had collected from Elmleigh, much to Claire's astonishment, since it was generally she herself who was dispatched to pick up culinary delicacies.

'I'm sure you're right,' was her innocent response, and Claire shot her a sharp look. What was Suzanne up to? Well, she could keep her hands off John Colby! 'You looked quite fierce then, Claire. Anyway, how is Martin?' Since Suzanne seemed genuinely interested, Claire told her as much as she thought was reasonable. Her vague replies seemed to satisfy her cousin, who concentrated on her chow mein while Claire merely picked at her meal before abandoning it. Somehow she had lost her appetite.

Perhaps finishing on Camber Ward had something to do with the heartache she was experiencing, she reflected as she washed up the plates afterwards. To her delight, Sister Whitelaw had organised a little leaving party for her, and the nurses clubbed together to buy her a pretty scarf. Tomorrow was a day off then at seven on Sunday morning it would be a new beginning for her. But it wasn't as if she would never see the consultant again. He was often on Westfield and——

No, she wasn't the slightest bit interested in seeing him again! Ruthlessly Claire scrubbed the plates, trying to convince herself that she had no more interest in John Colby than she had in David Dunster. Mr Dunster had, at least, said he was sorry she was moving, but as his gran had been discharged this afternoon Claire couldn't see that it would matter to him one way or the other.

Wendy seemed to be going along nicely since her discharge, and one of her daughters had been to see her, and Claire perked up a bit as she left the dishes to drain and switched the coffee on. They were off for a picnic in the park tomorrow, weather permitting, and Suzanne had promised to do all the organising and even the shopping for that, and Claire felt mean at even thinking she would be left to do it all yet again!

As it turned out, however, the wasps rather spoiled the picnic, since they were determined to get at the nectarines with which Suzanne had overloaded the picnic hamper, but the park wasn't too crowded and it was better than sitting in the jungle contemplating the gardening one ought to be doing.

'It was good of your Mr Colby to mow the lawn, wasn't it?' Suzanne spoke out of the blue, and Claire started. In her thoughts she had been with that same Mr Colby and she wondered uneasily whether Suzanne had realised how much of her spare time was taken up with dreaming about a certain tall, blue-eyed man.

'Yes, it was. I suppose it was a nice change from operating, though,' Claire reflected. 'He probably found it relaxing.'

'Probably,' Suzanne agreed lazily, then lay back against her cushion, stretching her long bare legs out in front of her. 'This saves money, doesn't it? A Mediterranean climate all of our own!'

'Mmm,' Claire said absently, then was about to close her eyes and go back to her daydreams when Suzanne gave a squeal of excitement. Claire shot up,

wondering what had prompted that unusual display of
emotion. The answer was coming across the grass
towards her — John Colby, picnic hamper in hand!

But he wasn't alone, and Claire assumed that the
young dark-haired girl with him was his daughter.
Well, hadn't she suspected he had a family tucked
away somewhere? *And* a wife? Just because he was
carrying on with Sister Pountney and Miss Wallace,
and had kissed a certain staff nurse, it didn't mean he
wasn't married. Even so, confirmation of this was
unwelcome, and Claire rose, self-consciously brushing
the crumbs from her rather ancient skirt, cross with
herself for doing so. Beside her, she heard Suzanne's
quick intake of breath, and understood the signs only
too well.

Suzanne, magnificent in emerald-patterned shorts,
was the first to speak, and Claire watched in exaspera-
tion as her cousin turned the charm full on. Poor John
Colby wouldn't stand a chance — poor *Mrs* John Colby,
she amended. 'You must be Mr Colby! Claire told me
there was a magnificent-looking man staying with the
Medhursts!' Suzanne trilled, then added with a coy
look, 'Actually she didn't. She thought you were a
jobbing gardener at first! Didn't you, pet?'

Numbly Claire nodded, then was even more disconcerted by John's wide grin. 'I liked the first description
better,' he commented, then urged the sullen-looking
girl forward. 'This is my daughter, Katy.'

Katy eyed them without speaking for a moment,
then muttered, 'Hello.' She looked to be about twelve
or thirteen, was about a head shorter than Claire, but
painfully thin, Claire gave her a warm smile, before
introducing her cousin. Suzanne and John shook
hands — shaking hands being a custom Suzannne never
bothered with normally — and before Claire knew
where she was the two parties had joined and Suzanne
was nudging her to help Katy set out the extra food.

Annoyed, Claire set to work silently, assisted by the
equally silent Katy. She didn't attempt to force conversation on the girl. She was probably a perfectly normal
chatty teenager when one got to know her. But *I* won't

be getting to know her—or her father, Claire decided, slapping away a wasp with unnecessary vigour.

'Daddy has that effect on women,' Katy said quietly, and a startled Claire swung round. There was a glint of humour in the girl's light eyes, and Claire's lips twitched.

'Suzanne has that effect on men, so we'll let them get on with charming each other, shall we?'

Suzanne and John were on first-name terms by now, and, having established eye contact with the surgeon, she turned her attention to his daughter. 'What are you finding to do in the school holidays, Katy? I expect you get bored with the long break. I know *I* always did,' Suzanne went on.

'I find things to do,' Katy said, obviously struggling to be polite.

'It's still boring, though, if you're left on your own a lot,' Suzanne persisted. 'I don't go back until Monday morning. You could always pop along to see us. Couldn't she, Claire?'

Surprised, Claire hastened to endorse the invitation, even knowing full well why it had been issued, but Katy merely shook her head. Then, when her father cocked an eyebrow, she coloured fiercely. 'Thank you, but I've really got loads to do.'

'Well, if you're ever at a loose end, you could come and help my cousin mow the lawn! We call the garden the jungle, don't we?' Not giving Claire time to answer, Suzanne hurried on, 'I work up in Town so it would have to be one weekend.' Then she stopped as if a thought had just struck her. 'Surely the schools haven't broken up yet? I haven't seen the hordes descending upon the village green!'

Claire noticed the way Katy was staring fixedly at the ground. 'Katy's in the procees of changing schools so she finished rather early,' John said easily, and all eyes turned to Katy, who began plucking at blades of grass with an intensity that worried Claire.

'You might as well enjoy the good weather now—it will probably rain all thorough August,' she said practically, and that broke the tension. It seemed to

Claire that the consultant's smile was approving, and
that the sun had doubled in strength during the last
few minutes.

'How long will you be in Elmleigh?' Suzanne asked,
as if aware that she had been out of the conversation
for too long. 'I know you're helping out until that
woman surgeon starts, but what then?' She leaned
forward, moving her legs slightly so that they were
displayed to their best advantage. Claire hid a smile,
but she could almost feel the resentment oozing out of
Katy.

John hesitated. 'I'm at the District until some time
in September. Then, like gypsies, we'll be off again.
Won't we, Katy? He smiled affectionately at his
daughter.

'Yes, new horizons, Daddy. Oh — you won't forget
what Mummy said about the boys, will you?'

'Ah!' He glanced at the watch on his tanned wrist.
'Yes, the boys. What was it Mummy said? Remind
me,' he said, while Suzanne paused, lemonade beaker
halfway to her lips and remaining there as if she'd been
frozen into immobility.

'About not letting them stay on the boating lake too
long,' Katy said slowly and distinctly. 'We ought to
pack up now — they'll be wondering where we are,'
she added, reinforcing her remark by tugging at her
father's hand.

Some silent message passed between father and
daughter, but only Claire was in a good position to see
it — yet, having seen it, she found it impossible to
interpret. She could interpret Suzanne's silence,
though. She was concentrating upon her drink but the
set of her shoulders indicated her shock. She had fallen
hard by the look of it, and Claire felt a momentary
spurt of anger against John. He had no business
charming the birds off the trees with that smile!

Wishing Mrs Colby would come to claim her husband and daughter, Claire rose and began packing the
picnic things away. 'Do you want to help, Katy? If
your brothers are waiting, it won't take so long if you
tidy and I pack,' she said, in a tone of voice her student

nurses would have recognised. But, to Staff Nurse Shaw's consternation, it was Katy's father who helped with the tidying, and she tensed, only too well aware of strong brown hands inches from her own. Her nostrils were assailed by a fresh, clean *male* scent, and a wave of longing overcame her. It was for Martin really, but in his arrogance John might have assumed she was overcome by *his* nearness, for when their hands met as they both reached for the tablecloth Claire jerked her hand away so swiftly that both he and Katy glanced at her in surprise. Hastily she scrambled up. 'We've made good time — your boys will still be on the lake, I expect.'

Suzanne had by now regained her composure, and had an artificial smile pinned to her lips. Claire's heart ached for her, but it was something to be chalked up to experience. The idea that some of the heartache might be for herself Claire dismissed. Of course she didn't care. Hadn't she told herself that a million times already?

Katy flashed Claire a big smile as they prepared to leave, but that mocking expression was back on her father's face, and Claire gave him a haughty look, trying to make him feel uncomfortable. Mrs Colby was more than welcome to him!

'I'm sorry we couldn't stay longer, but it was rather short notice.' John's level glance seemed to discomfit Suzanne, who merely shrugged, but Claire's sapphire eyes widened as she gazed from her cousin to the consultant and back again. Surely their meeting was no more than a coincidence?

'See you next week, Staff Nurse.' Father and daughter wandered off, sharing a joke by the sound of the girl's laughter, and Claire turned to Suzanne.

'What was short notice? You didn't invivte Mr Colby to meet us here, did you?' The answer was written on Suzanne's face, and Claire bit back the angry retort that was hovering on her lips. Typical!

'I phoned him while I was waiting for the take-away, but I didn't know he was bringing the entire family, if that's what you mean! How was I to know he had umpteen kids?' Suzanne sounded aggrieved, as well she might, and Claire decided to drop the subject.

'No, you couldn't have known,' she agreed quietly. 'Where to now?'

'I think we should treat ourselves to a cream tea — don't you?' Suzanne's smile was self-mocking. There was nothing Claire wanted less than a cream tea but it would at least take her mind off that disturbing encounter with John Colby. Quite why it was disturbing she wasn't yet prepared to analyse.

CHAPTER SEVEN

WESTFIELD was arranged much like Camber, in cubicles on an open-plan system, but had only twenty-four beds, shared between three consultants. 'Mr Colby's got the most beds, and his are mainly intestinal. One is query carcinoma but we're waiting for results — that's Tom Denny. He's in his eighties and everyone calls him Gramps. He's a real character, Claire.' Pam Fryer, the staff nurse, went on down the list while Claire hastily scribbled notes. What a lot there was to remember, and, knowing Sister Pountney, she would expect her deputy to be word-perfect by the following morning.

Pam's words echoed her thoughts. 'Stella's a bit of a perfectionist, but I get on all right with her. You'll need to know your stuff, though — make sure you can give her diagnosis, probable prognosis, and anything else you can remember!'

Claire sketched a salute. 'I'll do my best. Now I'd better meet them all. I'll miss my ladies, though,' she confided, as they toured the ward.

Apart from Mr Denny, two other patients had cancer, including George Upshall, whose prognosis was poor. John had deemed it worthwhile to operate shortly, though. The symptoms would be alleviated and the patient had previously been fit and active for his age. Claire was determined to find time to sit and talk with him. Mindful of John's textbook, she intended to check that her juniors understood what nurse-patient interaction meant, and that there was more required of them than just attention to the patients' physical needs.

Most of the men were up, several of them already congregating in the dayroom, or going to the lavatories, which were near the nurses' station. It was as Claire was passing these that she heard a faint cry for

91

help, and she and Staff Nurse Fryer dashed in, to find an elderly man trying to struggle to his feet.

'I must've slipped, Nurse. It's these floors — they're shiny!' His belligerent gaze fell upon Claire, who was hastily feeling for broken bones before they assisted him up. 'Who's this little gal, then?' he went on, giving her a gummy smile.

'I'm the new staff nurse, and if you *will* go to the toilet without your slippers on it's no wonder you slip about. Here, let me pull up your drawers while Nurse Pam finds your slippers,' Claire said sternly, and the patient smiled all the more.

'Here you are, Ted Tunstall, new slippers.' Pam eased his feet into them and together they walked him back to the ward, seating him by his bed. Fortunately he seemed none the worse for his fall, but it meant a call to the ward doctors and an accident form filled out. Mr Tunstall was almost ready for discharge after repair of his hernia, but Claire couldn't afford to take chances on an eighty-year-old patient, even though Pam thought a doctor's visit unnecessary.

'He'll be OK, Claire. Don't start fussing or Sister won't like it,' the older staff nurse advised. 'She's got the ward running like clockwork and patients like clockwork toys! They aren't supposed to fall about — it upsets the routine,' she went on, but Claire just smiled. She couldn't believe Stella Pountney put ward routine before patient care, and had the feeling Pam Fryer was testing her.

Mr Tunstall proved to be none the worse for his fall, and later Claire saw him in the dayroom taking part in what appeared to be a poker school! Probably something else Sister Pountney would disapprove of, she thought wryly as she went off for a quick lunch.

Since consultants never appeared on Sundays except in emergency, Claire was surprised to see a casually dressed John Colby on the ward when she returned. He was sitting by Tom Denny's bed, while the old man talked earnestly. She smiled to herself. John was a hit with old men as well as old ladies!

'I'm off to lunch, then,' Pam Fryer called, 'I'll be a

bit late back. Might as well while Stella's off. Good luck!' Then she was gone, leaving Claire with a ward full of patients she hardly knew, one part-time staff nurse who was eyeing her resentfully, and a couple of juniors who seemed to spend all their time scurrying here and there with bottles or commodes. The idea of sitting talking to patients was one Sister frowned upon, and Claire could see she would have her work cut out to personalise Westfield Ward. There was nothing like a challenge for easing a slight case of heartache!

'Is there some special reason for Mr Colby to be in today,' she asked Staff Nurse Rees, 'or is it his research?'

'I'm not sure, really. He often comes in when Sister's on,' Nurse Rees admitted with a sour smile. 'But Pam didn't say what he wanted today. Hadn't you better ask him?' With that, she headed for the office, leaving an exasperated Claire trying to remember that she enjoyed a challenge.

John glanced up as she approached, his eyes smiling at her. 'Here she comes, the guardian angel of Camber! You've met your new staff nurse, haven't you, Gramps? She got tired of the ladies and heard that you were a handsome young lad.' Since Mr Denny was rather deaf, the surgeon had to speak loudly, and the other men in the cubicle guffawed. One gave three rather weak cheers, and Claire grinned at them all. Perhaps life here wouldn't be so bad after all.

It hadn't taken Claire long to find out that Mr Denny was popular with the whole ward, and the younger men particularly always asked how he was, and he was affectionately known as Gramps by them as well as by the staff.

Claire didn't care to hear patients referred to as 'Gramps' or 'Dad' but in Mr Denny's case it was clearly a title he revelled in. Her eyes met the surgeon's across the bed. 'Is there anything I can do for you, sir? Staff Nurse Rees wasn't sure why you were on the ward and——'

'And Staff Nurse Fryer took off at the earliest possible moment and will be late back. Yes, I know the situation.' John spoke quietly so that the others couldn't hear. 'That's mainly why I suggested you be sent here, Claire. Westfield needs a dose of that cheery Nurse Shaw.'

'Oh!' Taken aback, Claire couldn't think of anything appropriate to say, so she beamed at him instead.

He grinned back, and Mr Denny's eyes went from one to the other. 'Your young lady, is she?' he bellowed at the surgeon, and Claire went pink as several heads swivelled towards them.

'I thought she was yours!' John said loudly, and the old man chuckled, giving Claire time to recover her poise. She treated the whole cubicle to what she hoped was a reproving glance, but the men just grinned back, and she gave up the attempt.

The surgeon rose, shook Mr Denny by the hand, then indicated to Claire that she should precede him to the office. 'You mustn't mind the patients, they're all boys at heart,' he said softly, speaking from just behind her, and Claire nodded automatically.

'Yes, sir,' she murmured as she opened the office door—to find Staff Nurse Rees reading a women's magazine. 'Perhaps you could keep an eye on the ward, Staff?' Claire suggested quietly, her tone of voice brooking no argument, and the red-faced nurse almost scurried out.

'You mustn't mind her either. I think she feels she should have been Sister's deputy, but Pam Fryer got there first,' John explained easily, sitting in the sister's chair and swivelling it around to face Claire.

'And now I'm taking over when Pam moves—yes, I can see she must be resentful,' acknowledged Claire, seating herself opposite him, after making sure that the office door was half-open. 'Though if she can't do full-time I'm afraid she hasn't much chance of getting on.'

He nodded, then leaned back wearily in the chair. 'It's been one hell of a week, Claire. I lost a patient yesterday on Hastings Ward—a dear old lady who should have died in a hospice, not here in a busy hospital. How's Wendy Clark? Are you keeping an eye on her?' Abruptly he seemed to switch subjects, but Claire sensed there was some connection between the two patients.

'She seems happy, and she's eating a bit. She's never had a great appetite,' she told him. 'Oh, and she's got a GP's appointment next Wednesday.'

'See that she keeps it — though I shouldn't ask you, should I? You seem to do enough running around after people.'

'Sometimes I do, but I like helping people. I wouldn't have become a nurse otherwise.' Some devil made her add, 'Not like Suzanne. I couldn't do *her* job. She seems to live either on a high or in the depths at work, as far as I can tell!'

'Yes, Suzanne. A charming lady.' John's tone was non-committal, then he grinned wickedly. 'I hope she wasn't too perturbed to find I had a family?'

'Er — she was a bit surprised, I think,' Claire prevaricated. 'You might like to bring your boys to play in the jungle. You've seen what it's like — plenty of places to hide from the enemy or play cops and robbers!'

'Perhaps one day I will. Thank you.' His tone was dismissive, then he turned the conversation to the men on the ward, giving Claire a surgeon's-eye view of them. 'Ted Tunstall can be discharged tomorrow, I think, but I'll get Gram to check that there's somewhere for him. The poor old chap lives alone,' John said, tapping the bed list.

'Mr Tunstall had a fall in the lavatory this morning,' Claire put in quickly. 'He's been examined and seems OK. He isn't looking forward to going home — he enjoys the company here!' she went on, mindful of the card game.

'Don't we all?' the surgeon said enigmatically. 'Joseph Hurst — in the same cubicle — he's a permanent colostomy, I'm afraid. An odd sort of man, isn't he? What's your opinion of him?' His gaze was penetrating, and Claire couldn't look away. For a moment, too, she couldn't recall that particular patient!

'Oh, Mr Hurst — yes. . . I can't say I've formed an opinion of him. He keeps very much to himself and seems to be gazing inwards all the time.' Claire went on to describe him fully, despite the briefness of her acquaintance with the man, then was pulled up by the surgeon's gentle laughter.

'For a nurse who hasn't formed an opinion of the patient, you're doing very well! Let's take a look at him together,' he suggested, 'before the hordes descend.'

Horrified, Claire glanced at her fob watch. Almost visiting time! 'I'd better check the other patients first, if you don't mind, see they're all ready for visitors.' Claire sped away, hurrying without actually seeming to. Several of the men remained in the dayroom but most had settled in chairs beside their beds, and Claire was relieved to see that Staff Nurse Rees hadn't been idle. The ward was reasonably tidy, all traces of lunch had been cleared away, and there were curtains drawn around only three beds. One of these, Claire saw, was Mr Hurst's.

He had been suffering from chronic obstruction of the bowel due to a tumour, and after operation had been left with a permanent colostomy, the large intestine or bowel being brought out through an opening in the abdominal wall, then cut across. The faeces drained into a special bag fixed to his abdomen, and Mr Hurst hadn't yet come to terms with this.

Claire stuck her head through a gap in the curtain, to find him sitting in bed, just gazing into space. 'Can I open the curtains now, Mr Hurst? It's nearly visitors.'

The patient, a short, thick-set man of sixty, looked up, his pale eyes lack-lustre. 'I don't want no visitors, Nurse. I'm busy thinking. Leave the curtains.' It was an order rather than a request, and Claire hesitated for a moment. If he wanted privacy, it seemed cruel to whisk back the curtains and expose him to the gaze of all and sundry, but it wasn't good for him to sit in solitary state looking inwards, dwelling on the prospect of wearing a colostomy bag for the rest of his life.

The dilemma was solved for her by John Colby, who proceeded to open the curtains. 'Hello, Mr Hurst. I wondered if you would mind helping me with the book

I'm writing? I expect you've seen me talking to the other patients.' With an easy smile, John sank into the easy-chair, which he turned slightly so that he could keep an eye on Mr Hurst.

'Oh, well, yes. Glad to help, doctor.' Claire noted with approval that Mr Hurst visibly perked up at being asked for help, and she was reluctant to leave, but it was dead on two and the visitors would be champing at the bit.

Then Pam Fryer came back, less than ten minutes late and full of apologies, so Claire decided to say nothing to her. A new broom sweeping clean on her first day would certainly be resented. Time enough for that when she had sussed out the situation here — and formed some sort of rapport with Stella Pountney!

'Yes, you seem to have a good grasp of the routine.' Sister Pountney's tone was gracious, almost pleased, and Claire silently breathed a sigh of relief. The first hurdle over! This was Monday morning, the night staff had gone, and Sister had invited Claire to brief her on the previous day's happenings. She also wanted chapter and verse for each patient, much as Pam Fryer had said she would, and Claire was pleased that she'd been able to meet those expectations.

'We should get confirmation about Tom Denny today,' Sister was saying, and Claire nodded.

'The other patients keep an eye on him, I've noticed — you would think he was their grandfather!'

'That's what I like to see. If they can take an interest in someone else's symptoms, they don't keep complaining about their own,' Sister said drily, then sat back in her chair, light eyes surveying Claire unsmilingly. 'I have to say that I didn't really want you on my ward,' she began. 'I thought you were just another pretty face, to be honest,' she went on relentlessly before Claire could find her tongue. 'And you look so young!' She made it sound like a dreadful disease, and Claire nearly lost her temper, remembering just in time to count to ten. 'But John persuaded Upstairs to have a change around and I think he was right. We all

get stale being on one ward too long. Even sisters,'
she confessed.

'Yes, I'm sure you're right,' Claire said carefully.
'As a matter of fact, *I* didn't want to come here. I got
settled on Camber, knew the routine, the patients, but
. . .it's all good experience — I can see that now.'

'So neither of us got what we wanted, but never
mind,' Sister finished briskly, getting up and adjusting
the navy belt around her incredibly slender waist,
before gliding away.

George Upshall was calling to Claire even before
she approached his bed. 'Got a minute, have you? I
keep forgetting what that sister says to me. Run
through it again, will you, love?'

Claire helped herself to a chair and settled herself
by the bed, but no sooner had she done so than Sister
appeared and beckoned. George sighed gustily, and
Claire felt like following suit, but managed not to as
she followed the sister to the nurses' station.

'We can't waste time sitting by patients' beds, Staff
Nurse. Mondays are always busy and——'

'Mr Upshall wanted reassurance, Sister,' Claire
broke in, 'I certainly wasn't wasting time. We're here
for the patients, after all.' There, now she had well
and truly burned her boats!

Stella Pountney's lips tightened. 'That may be how
Sister Whitelaw goes on, but on Westfield we have
different rules! You may sit and talk to him *after* we've
got through the morning's work, not before.'

Claire bridled, but, before she said something she
would certainly regret, John and Gram made their
appearance and she was able to slip away. Sister
wouldn't want her around now the consultant was on
the ward!

After a quick word of apology to Mr Upshall and a
promise to return later, Claire busied herself with the
morning's routine. It didn't vary much from Camber
but she was glad to see that Stella Pountney insisted
on two nurses doing the medicine round, something
Sister Whitelaw was rather lax about. Even discount-
ing the risk of giving out the wrong medication if one

nurse worked alone, Claire felt that the learners ought to have the opportunity of assisting at the round.

There were two learners at the moment, and Claire tried to put them at their ease, since they seemed to be suffering from shattered nerves! 'First check the medication against the patient's card, read the label, then check with another nurse that you *are* about to give what's perscribed,' Claire intoned as she began the round. 'What comes next?' she asked with a smile, and the first-year looked blank for a moment, her scared eyes on Claire's face. 'Yes?' Claire prompted. 'Take your time, no one's rushing you.'

'Sister will be,' the junior mumbled. 'Oh, I know! Check that you've giving it to the right patient. Ask him his name or check his wristband.' At Claire's smiling nod, she did so, and the round progressed slowly, Claire teaching all the while. Unfortunately the round was too slow for the ward sister, who sent Staff Nurse Rees to see what was causing the hold-up.

'I'm doing a bit of teaching as I go around,' Claire said crisply. 'Don't you like to teach?'

The other nurse hesitated, 'I would if I got the chance,' she admitted, and Claire gave her a warm smile.

'You're welcome to do some teaching when I'm here. It will take me a few weeks to get into the swing of things,' Claire confessed. 'Does Sister want me for anything specific?' She stood by the trolley, wondering whether this was to be the pattern of her days: get started on one procedure then be called to heel. Well, it wouldn't work! She wasn't a sheepdog.

'Mr Colby wanted a word with you, I think. Shall I put the trolley away?'

'Yes, please. Oh, and take Nurse Stebbins with you; she's keen to learn.' Claire handed over the keys and sped away. It was unfortunate if John Colby wanted to speak to her under the eagle eyes of a certain Miss Pountney!

He was in the office, sprawling at his ease, long legs stretched lazily out in front of him. 'Come in, Staff Nurse! I was telling Stella that we've started the patient sessions on Camber and that you think they're a good thing.' Did she imagine it, or was John's smile mocking her?

Deciding to play him at his own game, Claire smiled sweetly at them both. 'They seemed to go down well, sir. Are you starting sessions on Westfield?'

'Mmm, I think so—if we have this lady's permission?' John turned his smile full on, and Claire could almost see the sister melt in the heat.

'You know how to get your own way,' Sister said drily. 'I've no objection, but you know what Upstairs are saying.'

'What are they saying?' Claire put in, and Sister raised a thinly pencilled brow.

'Haven't you heard on the grapevine? New broom sweeps clean, he's only passing through, he's got no right to do his research here—that sort of thing. I suppose when Tania comes she'll continue with this?'

'You can bet on that,' John said softly, then chuckled. 'A very determined lady is Tania Wallace!' He got up, his gaze switching to Claire, who was trying to be invisible by the door. 'Katy was asking after you. I think she enjoyed the picnic, though with Katy it's difficult to know.' His tone was wry.

'She's welcome to call into the jungle any time she wants, especially if she likes plants. I've decided to grow a few in pots, and——' Claire began, but stopped at Sister's incredulous expression.

'I doubt if Mr Colby's daughter is interested in pot-plants! Anyway, run along and have a think about suitable patients, will you?' She smiled a dismissal, and Claire thankfully left them to it. Really, that woman was turning into more of a *That Woman* than Miss Wallace!

Sister was, thankfully, off at four so Claire had the last hour or so in sole charge. It was amazing how the atmosphere changed once their senior had departed, and even the harassed students relaxed.

George Upshall had his wife visiting, and, mindful of her promise, Claire went over to speak to him. Mrs Upshall looked as worried as her husband and Claire tried to ease her mind. 'Your husband was asking about the op, Mrs Upshall,' she began. 'Do you want to ask me anything while I've got a minute?'

'While that sister's off, she means,' George said to his wife in what he obviously thought was a whisper, but it carried all round the cubicle, and Claire just hoped it wouldn't reach a certain pair of ears the following day!

'Is it bad, Staff Nurse?' his wife asked, her tightly clenched hands indicative of her tension. 'Sister and Mr Colby said it had got a hold on George.'

'It' was carcinoma of the stomach, and Claire was able to tell them that it hadn't advanced so far that nothing could be done. 'We have great confidence in our Mr Colby,' she went on. 'He wouldn't lie to you — if he thought there was no point in an operation, he'd tell you.' Claire knew that the couple realised an operation was the last chance for George. It would make it possible for him to eat normally again and remain well for some time to come. And, as John had explained to the nurses, miracles did happen. It wasn't up to any surgeon to say there was no hope. If the patient was a fighter, there was always hope.

'They're taking away part of me stomach — that right, Nurse?'

'Yes, it's called a partial gastrectomy, but they won't take out more than they need to, and you'll still have enough left to put food into! You'll need to take small meals once you're back on solids — half as much food, twice as often, perhaps. Your theatre nurse is coming up tomorrow to meet you, and she'll be there when you have your op, and someone from this ward will take you to Theatre. So you'll have two nurses you know.'

Claire explained a little more about the pre-op preparation, then left them to continue their conversation. Something was nagging at the back of her mind, though, and it wasn't until she was changing her uniform after duty that she realised what it was: George Upshall's symptoms were similar to Wendy Clark's. Was that the clue John had been looking for?

Deep in thought, Claire emerged from the side-entrance, glad to feel the cool breeze against her body. A little rain had actually fallen during the night, but despite the coolness she felt drained, weary. The sound of a husky chuckle broke into her reverie, and she glanced over to the senior side of the car park. Yes, there was the Mercedes, but this time the consultant wasn't alone. Tania Wallace was beside him, and, even as she watched, Claire saw him put his arm around his colleague and hug her. Well! Evidently he made a habit of making love in the car park.

Trying to be invisible once again, Claire made her way by a roundabout route to her own car. So much for that kiss. The man was a Bluebeard! How many was that now? There was Tania Wallace and Sister Pountney. . . Oh, and what about Student Nurse Wise? Carefully reversing out of her space, Claire put all all such thoughts from her mind, or tried to. Like Martin, John was also slipping from his pedestal.

Tuesday was a dreadful day on Westfield, and once she was home Claire relived some of the worst points. Sister, for some reason, had decided to move the beds around. The men liked to stay with their bed-neighbours and resented being moved. One of them, Kevin Blake, had the temerity to tell her so, and clearly it had been a considerable shock to Sister Pountney, who had taken to the office and not emerged until going-home time!

Just after that, John had strolled on to the ward and, instead of presenting himself at the office and waiting for Sister to accompany him, had asked Claire to do so. It gave her an opportunity to speak to him about Wendy and her continued lack of appetite. To her chagrin, John hadn't thought it relevant.

'*Sudden* loss of appetite is a significant factor, but, after all, Wendy has never had much appetite — you said so yourself,' he pointed out gently, then reached across and adjusted that awful cap, which was wobbling again. Sister saw them from her sanctuary and Claire could feel eyes boring into her back all the way through the ward.

Then John went into the office while a distraught Claire did the medicine round, supervised the dressings, spoke to visitors, accompanied a visiting clergyman and answered his questions, and did virtually everything else, or so it seemed. John had the learners into the office for an impromptu teaching session, Staff Nurse Rees had gone off sick, and that left Claire and Pam Fryer to hold the fort.

Claire was just adjusting a bleeping drip when one of the juniors came with a message that Sister wanted to speak to her, and, glancing at her watch, Claire saw with horror that it was nearly five, and she wasn't finished yet.

She presented herself at the office, determinedly keeping a cheerful expression on her face, though it wasn't easy. Her feet were hot and aching due to the amount of running about she'd had to do, her face was flushed because John's touch, impersonal though it was, had set her pulses over-reacting as usual, and she just knew Sister was going to wipe the floor with her!

Sister Pountney was obviously a past master at emotional torture, for she began by discussing the ward routine, the operations list, and the duty rota, reeling off facts and figures so fast that Claire had a job to keep up with her. No mention was made of the surgeon until Claire, laden with lists, was about to leave the office.

That cool voice stopped her in her tracks. 'You came with Sister Whitelaw's highest recommendation, Staff, but. . .' Sister allowed her voice to trail off, and Claire spun round, sapphire eyes innocent.

'Yes, Sister?' They traded glances, and it was the other woman's eyes that slid away.

'It isn't helpful if you try to monoplise a consultant, Nurse Shaw,' Sister tried again, but Claire remained silent. 'John is friendly, I know, and some people might get the wrong idea. I wouldn't want you to get hurt.' She sat back, her face expressionless.

'No, Sister,' Claire said, then relented. 'What were you trying to say, exactly? I have to speak to Mr Colby sometimes.'

'Yes, but. . .he *is* a consultant and——'

'And married—yes, I know,' Claire said crisply, and Sister Pountney's eyes widened. Surely she knew that already? John couldn't have kept at least three children *and* a wife secret from Stella Pountney! No, not when they were so obviously lovers.

'Ah, I wasn't sure whether you knew.' Was there relief in Sister's voice? Or was it amusement? 'He and I are good friends, but I understand the situation.' She shrugged.

Claire contented herself with a murmured, 'Yes, Sister,' before leaving the office, fuming.

What did Sister take her for? They both understood the situation only too well! John Colby had a wife and family *and* he was playing the field. What else was there to understand? Yet. . . Claire had the feeling that somewhere along the line she might have misjudged him. He didn't seem the philandering type. But nor did Martin, she pointed out to herself as she sped around the ward, trying to finish before suppers and evening visitors. At this rate she would still be on duty when the night staff arrived. . .

Shuddering at the memory, Claire stared unseeingly at the television now. Another day like that and there wouldn't be enough of her left to yearn for the philandering John Colby!

Next day was a late duty, and Claire was talking to Jill Murray as they strolled across from the car park when a familiar voice hailed her. She turned slowly, to see Martin just leaving his car.

'Ah, the lord of the manor!' Jill giggled. 'He still hangs around, then? Be good!' She hurried away, leaving Claire to greet Martin reluctantly. She just hoped no one else would get the wrong idea.

'Hello, Claire. Sorry—am I keeping you?' Martin didn't sound sorry, but then he never did. 'I thought you might like to come home—back to the manor for a meal, perhaps?'

'I'm going *on* duty, not off,' she said calmly. 'I won't be finished until half-nine, and it will be ten before I emerge into the fresh air.' If there's enough of me left to emerge, she thought wryly.

'Yes, of course — I didn't think. Tomorrow, perhaps? Jessica's dying to see you again and I — '

'She can come to see me at home, can't she?' Claire suggested. Jessica was Martin's sister and several years younger than Claire. They hadn't really been friends and there wasn't any reason why they should want to see each other again. But Mr and Mrs Medhurst had been surrogate parents and Claire would have liked to call to see them, though they had spoken on the telephone. Only the thought of meeting Martin there had prevented her from paying them a visit. That, and the possibility that she would meet the mysterious Mrs Colby!

'You aren't saying much but you're obviously thinking deeply,' Martin said with an easy smile. 'Jessica's going through a bad patch and I thought you might cheer her up. Boyfriend trouble — you know the sort of thing.'

'Yes, I *do* know the sort of thing.' Claire's tone was icy. 'I can hardly drop in just like that. What about all four of you coming for a meal at my house some time? It will have to be on one of my days off, though.'

'Yes, OK, but I thought I could turn to you, Claire. You're the only one who understands!' Martin took hold of her hands and held on, despite Claire's attempts to free herself. 'I'm so depressed about Jacinth I don't know whether I'm coming or going!'

'Ring her, then. Tell *her* you're missing her,' Claire suggested, managing at last to free her hands. 'Look, I'm going to be late on duty and Sister's a bit of a battleaxe. Let me know what your parents say about lunch one day.'

Martin's mournful voice followed her. 'I could give the Samaritans a bell, I suppose.'

Claire turned, wishing she had time to count to a hundred rather than ten. It was Mrs Medhurst who had taught her to count to ten before exploding, she recalled. Perhaps Martin's mother realised how trying her son could be!

'I'm sure the Samaritans have enough to do, Martin!
Don't be such a fool.' Claire's voice was sharper than
she had intended, and he looked stunned. It was time
someone spoke sharply to him. All through his life he
had been spoiled, having only to beckon for people to
rush to do his bidding. Including me, Claire silently
acknowledged, that youthful, besotted creature that
was Claire Shaw. Now he must do something for
himself. 'Let me know about lunch, anyway.' She
raised a hand in farewell, then let it drop suddenly,
her face ashen.

Emerging from the A and E entrance was John
Colby, shepherding his daughter, who had a bandaged
hand. With them was Tania Wallace. Even as Claire
watched, Katy turned to say something to Miss
Wallace, who ruffled her hair affectionately.

A shaken Claire hurried towards the stairs. Seeing
Katy and the lady surgeon side by side, the resem-
blance was unmistakable. Now she knew who Tania
Wallace was—Mrs John Colby!

CHAPTER EIGHT

CLAIRE stumbled through the week somehow, mainly by ruthlessly keeping her mind on nursing matters, even when she was off-duty. She absolutely refused to think about charismatic consultants, expecially about one with a wife and three children. How *could* he?

With the man himself she was cool and polite, confining herself to taking his instructions and offering her comments when asked — and sometimes when not — on the patients and their nursing care. Mr Denny was discharged since he had presented himself for treatment too late, and there was nothing that could be done for his pancreatic cancer. But George Upshall had come out of his op successfully, though the surgeons had been drained and weary after coming from Theatre. Even the stiletto-tongued Gram had been silent, and Claire's soft heart had gone out to them both, despite everything.

When John did a round after Theatre, the steely-eyed stranger was back, and Claire knew it was because the operation had been a difficult one and hadn't been a cure. But it had certainly relieved George's symptoms, making what life was left to him more bearable. Joe Hurst, too, was making progress, and seemed to have come to terms with his colostomy bag. A member of the Colostomy Association had been to visit him, to discuss his future life with a colostomy, and Claire felt he had derived a great deal of benefit from speaking with someone who had worn such a bag for years and hadn't let it interfere with his normal life.

One more shift then days off, Claire thought thankfully a couple of days later. Sister was on a late for once, and that lightened the atmosphere on Westfield, though now Claire had got to know her better she realised what a good nurse Stella Pountney was. She

cared as much about the patients as Sister Whitelaw,
and even her brusque manner no longer bothered
Claire quite as much.

Now, a quick assessment of the patients before the
breakfast trolley came trundling along. Those men
who could had washed themselves and shaved, though
the barber would be along mid-morning to attend to
the three men who couldn't manage, George among
them.

The new patient would need a friendly word, Claire
decided, once she'd seen the others. Strictly speaking,
he didn't belong on their ward, but there was no room
anywhere else. She fervently hoped he would be
moved soon, and she could hear him moaning as she
reached his cubicle. Then came Bert Ferguson's gruff
voice. 'For pity's sake, shut up, will yer? There's
enough noise in this blo——' Bert paused as Claire
arrived, then threw up his hands in a helpless gesture.

Claire's lips twitched as she wagged a disapproving
finger at him. 'No swearing, Bert — you'll be filling that
swear box by yourself if you're not careful!' Bert, who
had undergone a herniotomy, was due for discharge
later that morning, and they would miss his coarse
humour! Tad Dean was in a different category, and,
despite feeling sorry for the boy, Claire would heave a
sigh of relief when he was transferred to Rye Ward, in
the genito-urinary unit.

This didn't show in her face as she walked purpose-
fully up to his bed. 'I won't ask how you are this
morning because that's obvious, but the night nurse
said you'd had a good night.' Claire settled herself by
the eighteen-year-old Tad's bed and took his hand,
her fingers feeling automatically for his pulse. Under
her touch, he lay quiescent, the agony apparently
evaporating as swiftly as it had come, and she raised a
brow. 'A bit easier now, is it?' she asked, and Tad
nodded.

'Yeah. It comes and goes, right? It goes down to me
private parts, Nurse,' he hissed, causing muted
chuckles from the other men.

Then Bert piped up, 'He wants you to do a complete

physical examination of his private parts, ducks! We'll chaperon you!'

Straight-faced, Claire whisked the curtains about the bed, then stuck her head out and said softly, 'If you don't control yourself, Bert Ferguson, I'll send you to the vets!'

The loud laughter from the men could be heard as far as the ward office, Claire felt sure, but renal colic was no joking matter. 'Your pulse has settled down nicely, Tad. Are you in pain at this moment?' He had been on pethidine overnight, but Claire didn't want him to have more if an analgesic would be sufficient, as it ought to be once the severe colicky pain had passed.

Tad, a thin, undersized youth, started to say yes, then, under Claire's watchful gaze, turned it into a 'No'. 'It's gone off now, darling, but I can't keep drinking that stuff.' He pointed to the water jug on his locker. 'I could do with a beer.' His voice was wistful, but he didn't protest when Claire shook her head.

'You must try to drink three litres over the period of a day and night, Tad, and you aren't. Tap water isn't anything special, I know, but have you got anyone who can bring you in spring water? Or you can have squash, if you'd prefer? Barley water?'

Tad pulled a face. 'Barley water! God, no. I'll just lie here for a while, I think.' But even that was to be denied him.

'When the pain's eased a bit, you have to get up and about, Tad. Exercise might help dislodge the stone. You know that and——' Claire began, then a head was thrust through the curtains and she swung round to meet the disapproving gaze of John Colby.

'No one seemed to know where you were, Acting Sister,' he said pointedly, and Claire flushed. 'Then we all heard raucous laughter and I simply followed the sound,' John went on with grim humour.

To Claire's dismay, Tad made a bad situation worse by grabbing her hand and holding on to it. 'You leave Nurse Claire alone! She's better than that prissy-faced sister! She don't like me, but Claire does—don't you?'

His anxious gaze was fixed on Claire, who noted in passing that his eyes were the same intense blue as a certain consultant's!

'Right, Tad,' she said firmly, getting up, 'but Sister Pountney doesn't dislike you. She's merely keen to see you get to another ward where they have the expertise — *and* more nurses.'

'That will be this afternoon, Staff Nurse. Get up now, Tad,' John went on, and under that stern eye the boy gingerly swung his legs out of bed, Claire supporting him as he stood. He wasn't much taller than she, and she got him into his dressing-gown and bright red slippers while the surgeon whisked back the bed-curtains.

Leaving Tad sitting grumpily by his bed, water jug at hand, Claire followed John meekly enough, but her anger wasn't as well concealed as she hoped, for he ushered her into the office and closed the door firmly behind them.

'That young man thrives on attention, Claire — particularly from a lovely young nurse and — '

'Thank you for the compliment,' Claire broke in, pleased despite her annoyance at the way she had been shepherded from Tad's bedside. 'He hasn't got designs on me, and he *was* in pain,' she pointed out, this remark being greeted by a raised brow.

'Pulse-rate?' he asked softly, and Claire had to admit it was within Tad's normal limits. 'Pallor? Sweating?' John went on conversationally, his questions drawing a reluctant smile from Claire.

'No, he wasn't in pain,' she admitted, 'but he needs attention. He lives with his granny and — '

John stopped her by putting his hands on her shoulders, the warmth seeping even through the thick uniform dress, and Claire tensed. 'Claire, you can't open your tender heart to *all* of them. Your job is to supervise the ward in the absence of the ward sister, *and* keep a keen look-out for wandering consultant surgeons. What do I find when I *do* wander in? An acting sister nowhere in sight, the other nurses fully occupied with getting out breakfasts, the junior left to

cope with a vomiting patient,' he went on remorselessly, 'and you having a heart-to-heart with a patient
who will soak up every ounce of people's sympathy
then keep coming back for more. I know colic is
painful, but it's intermittent, and for the painful phases
he's written up for a strong drug.'

To Claire's mingled relief and dismay, he let her go,
and now there was a faint smile on his face as he
settled himself comfortably in Sister Pountney's chair,
pulling it back so that he could rest his feet on the said
sister's desk. 'Go and supervise your ward, Staff
Nurse, and leave one weary surgeon to write up notes.
I want Tad's bed for my new admission when Rye
have taken him. Or I might need it for myself — how
about joining me?' he invited, his smile deepening.

Claire fled, not trusting herself to speak. Sharing a
hospital bed with John Colby wasn't such a bad idea!

Her eagerly awaited time off finally came around
again. Tad had duly been transferred, protesting
loudly that he wanted to stay on Westfield. The new
admission hadn't yet been transferred from Theatre,
what had started out as an 'acute abdomen' in for
investigations having turned into a full-blown peritonitis. Sister would cope with him, though, and Claire
was glad to be relieved of that responsibility.

Now, after a restless night, she flopped down on to
the settee and gazed miserably out at the light rain.

For once, Suzanne hadn't returned to Hemsley
Green, so Claire had invited Jill Murray and a few
other nurses around after work and they'd held an
impromptu party. The clearing-up remained to be
done but at least the party hadn't been anything like
Suzanne's!

That lady had been evasive on the telephone when
Claire had asked her why she was remaining up in
London. 'Reggie's been invited to a simply marvellous
party, Claire, and he's asked me along. Anyway, the
village will still be there next weekend,' she had said
blithely. It was obvious to Claire, though, that had
John Colby proved to be single Reggie's marvellous
party could have taken place without her cousin!

Claire nudged a paper napkin with her foot, knowing she really ought to begin tidying, but lacking the incentive. There was always tomorrow. . . Heavens, she was beginning to sound slovenly! Rousing herself, she jumped up then began on the living-room.

She was just vacuuming the carpet when the doorbell rang, and for a moment she was tempted not to answer it. It might be Martin. True, she hadn't seen or heard anything of him since that awful day when she had discovered the truth about the Colbys, but who else could it be?

It proved to be Katy, who stood awkwardly on the doorstep, an anxious expression on her face. Claire gave her a warm smile — this was one of the Colbys she *could* welcome! 'Come in — how's your hand?'

'Oh, it's all right, thank you.' Katy followed her into the living-room, then allowed Claire to inspect her hand, which had only a small dressing on it now. 'I cut it quite badly in the garden, but you would think I'd caught AIDS or something, the fuss Mummy made!' Head on one side, she surveyed Claire as if trying to assess how she would take this information.

'You have to think of tetanus, that's why Mummy was concerned.' Claire's voice was brisk, professional. 'I saw you and your parents coming out of A and E the other day, and I wondered what you'd done. Do you want coffee? I was just going to sit down for a while.'

They sat companionably on the settee while Claire mentally took stock of Katy. She looked thinner than ever and Claire only hoped she wasn't anorexic. John had enough to put up with without that and —— Oh, bother, John! She hadn't meant to think about him ever again, but how difficult that was proving.

'Daddy said I could come and see the jungle,' Katy volunteered, after she had finished her coffee and three biscuits. Not anorexia nervosa, then, Claire noted with relief.

'Yes, of course. You can help me keep the weeds under if you like — perhaps on a better day. And the boys, if they want to come,' Claire rushed on, wondering why she was tormenting herself. A little boy like John would be rather nice. Slim-built with intensely blue eyes and an engaging smiling and —

'Oh, yes, my brothers — I've got two, you know.' Katy's gaze was almost fierce. 'Robert's ten and Johnnie's — ' She paused, then shrugged. 'I can't quite remember. I think he's coming up to eight now. He's taller than Robert and I sometimes forget which one is the elder,' she hurried on, seeing Claire's puzzled expression.

'That often happens. Probably Robert will shoot up suddenly, then he'll be the taller one — I shouldn't worry if he's undersized.' This remark provoked a fit of giggles though Claire couldn't see why. No doubt all would be revealed if ever she met the boys. But she didn't need to, for Katy went on about them at such length that Claire felt she would know them instantly. Robert was going to follow in their parents' footsteps but Johnnie was definitely going to be a farmer.

'Or maybe a vet — I hadn't thought of that,' Katy mused, then flushed. 'Shall I help you clear up?'

Claire wasn't about to turn down an offer of help, so she got on with the vacuuming while Katy washed the cups then wielded a duster to such good effect that Claire told her she hadn't seen the house looking so neat and tidy for a few weeks. 'I just do the minimum, I'm afraid,' Claire explained, as she emptied the cleaner. 'It's not raining now — do you want to see over the jungle? Or is Mummy expecting you back?'

To her dismay, Katy burst into tears, and it was a little while before the sad story emerged: Daddy and Mummy didn't live together any more, and it was with Daddy she was staying at present. She did, however, have a bright idea for the future — Nurse Claire Shaw could bring them together again!

Aghast, Claire could only stare. She could feel herself colour and knew that Katy's eyes hadn't missed that. 'It they're separated, it's no one else's business but theirs,' she begun, not sure if Katy would listen to reason. 'I can't interfere — no one can. Anyway, they clearly get on well and — '

'Yes, they do!' Eagerly Katy caught at her hand. 'They just need a little push in the right direction, that's all. I *want* to be a family again!'

'What about the boys? Do they live with Mummy?' It seemed an odd arrangement. And what about Miss Wallace's bereavement? She was supposed to have lost her husband!

'Yes, they do at the moment. I used to but. . .' Katy hesitated, then confided with a bright smile, 'I got expelled from school and Daddy said Mummy spoilt me and I'd have to stay with him for a while.'

'Expelled?' Claire tried not to show her surprise.

'Well, not quite expelled,' the girl amended, 'but very nearly. Mummy's been concentrating on her career, and Daddy was going abroad, so he cancelled that and came here instead.'

'I thought——' Claire began, then decided against mentioning Miss Wallace's bereavement. It might seem as if she was prying. 'You've got a longer holiday than usual, then, so you'd better make the most of it. Do some studying, or go on educational trips, perhaps,' she went on, and Katy pulled a face.

'You sound like Daddy,' she complained, and Claire smiled.

'If I hadn't studied pretty hard, I wouldn't have been allowed even to *start* my nursing training, let alone finish it. My dad would have been so proud of me,' Claire went on, 'and I'm sure yours will be proud of you when you go to university, or. . . What *do* you want to do, anyway? You've talked about the boys and their future but not your own.'

'Oh, it's easy to talk about the boys,' Katy said airily. 'I'm not sure about me. Mummy said I ought to have some idea by now but I haven't.' Blue eyes surveyed Claire. Then she smiled, the likeness to her mother still remarkable, but that smile was pure John Colby!

'Are you and Martin lovers? Daddy thinks so,' Katy observed a little later as they ate a snack meal in the kitchen.

Taken aback, Claire carefully cut her pasty into

small pieces before replying. 'Martin was my boyfriend a long time ago. We grew up together, but he's married now. Married men are all past and no future—that's what my cousin says. You met her at the picnic—Suzanne, the glamorous blonde!'

'Oh, that one! She fancied Daddy but she went off him when I mentioned the boys, didn't she?' Katy sounded gleeful.

'I don't think she fancied him,' Claire said hesitantly, 'but he's an attractive man, and Suzanne's only human, after all. She's actually got a boyfriend up in London. She's here only at weekends, and not always then.'

'That's all right—I didn't want her to fancy herself as Daddy's next wife!'

Claire looked her surprise. 'But he's married! They're only separated, you told me—didn't you?'

'Well, no, they aren't married now—they're divorced. But they'll soon get together again, and you can help, Claire, please! You're on his ward and——'

'No! I told you, I'm not playing matchmaker for *anybody*! If they want to try marriage again, that's up to them. Just show them both you love them and would feel happier, more secure, if they remarried. That ought to help,' Claire advised, wondering why she was acting as agony aunt. She needed one herself!

There was hostility in Katy's eyes now. 'I expect you're right. I'll tell them I'd do better at school if they got married again, shall I?' Then she jumped up. 'I'd better go—Mrs Taylor gets worried if I'm out too long. You'd think I was a child!' As Katy had previously admitted that she had just had her twelfth birthday, Claire was inclined to the same view as the Medhursts' housekeeper. Hemsley Green was a peaceful village, but there was no point in taking risks.

'I'll see you tomorrow, if it's fine. We might have a picnic on the terrace, if you like?' Claire suggested, as she set Katy down within sight of the manor's front door, but though Katy thanked her politely it wasn't with any real enthusiasm.

One could hardly blame her, Claire reflected—a

picnic with a grown-up in a garden was hardly an exciting prospect to a twelve-year-old girl. She was at the in-between stage, that was the trouble, and there was nothing for her age-group in the village except for the church youth club and—— No, Staff Nurse Shaw, you aren't taking responsibility for any more lame ducks! Let the Colbys look after their own daughter *and* sort out their marital problems! With that firm intention, Claire drove back to a bleakly empty house. It was strange, but her future also seemed bleak and empty.

She took Wendy Clark out for a drive in the country the following morning, even though it was still overcast. Now that her family had temporarily stopped their bickering and had gathered around her, Wendy seemed happier though still preoccupied, perhaps with morbid thoughts. 'Do you see anyone from the hospital now, Wendy?' Claire asked, as they drove past the church and past the lane which would have taken them to the manor and Martin Medhurst.

'Funny you should say that, Claire. When I was in that Camber Ward, I spotted an old friend—he's a patient in the annexe—and we had a good old chin-wag. Me daughters don't approve, though,' she added morosely, and Claire's eyes widened. This was certainly news. Perhaps this was the man she'd seen Wendy with. And, if she was pining for this man's company, it went some way to explaining her listlessness and lack of appetite.

When invited to talk about him, Wendy did so with such animation that Claire turned the car and headed towards the Elmleigh District. In the psychiatric unit there was usually open visiting, despite the disapproval of Upstairs, and soon Wendy and her friend, Sam, were sitting in the dayroom, leaving Claire free for at least an hour.

Deciding to pop into the canteen in the general hospital, Claire was just picking up a tray when John Colby came striding up to her. 'Coming in on your days off, Staff Nurse?' he enquired.

'No, I just dropped Wendy Clark at the annexe and

I've got to hang about while she visits someone. A friend,' Claire rushed on, and John smiled.

'Don't look so fierce, Claire — I'm not going to scold you!' His smile deepened as he joined her in the queue. To her consternation, he followed her to the table, setting down his cup of tea and packet of biscuits beside hers. 'You don't object?' Claire almost said she did but thought better of it. There was no point in provoking him unnecessarily.

'Feel free,' she said instead, then busied herself stirring her tea, keeping her eyes down.

'How is Wendy?' Thankfully the surgeon's conversation was neutral, and Claire told him about Sam. 'He's an old friend and Wendy wants to see more of him,' Claire went on, waving her teaspoon to emphasise a point.

'Is she any better physically, do you think?' John asked, his eyes intent on her face.

Claire started to nod, then shook her head instead. 'I suppose that means I'm not sure! She just pecks at her food but her GP said it wasn't anything to worry about at first. Now she's got a fortnightly appointment and I pop in when I can. Oh, and the district nurse — she's been several times, and the community psychiatric nurse. So everyone is rallying round.'

'Don't get too involved, Claire — you must have enough to do. I'll ask Katy to come and give you a hand with that jungle some time. I gather she invited herself around yesterday, but don't let her become a burden,' John said quietly. 'You're so kind-hearted that people take advantage of you — I don't like to see that.'

John's eyes were kind, concerned, but Claire would really have preferred to see a spark of passion in them, if she were honest with herself. She didn't want him to be concerned, though it was a long time since anybody had been. Oh, she didn't know what she wanted, and that was a fact!

'Claire?' he prompted, that mocking little smile breaking out, and she took a sip of tea before replying.

'I don't think people take advantage of me, no. But

I like caring; it's the reason I became a nurse,' she said coolly, wondering how he would react if she reached across the table and stroked the lean, tanned hand which was just reaching for a biscuit!

'How is Westfield Ward?' Was there a purpose behind that question? Claire wondered. What John probably meant was How are you coping with Sister Pountney?

'Not as interesting as Camber, but I'm managing.' She looked him straight in the eye, then they both started to laugh.

'Yes, I believe you are,' was John's only comment, but Claire bathed in the warm glow of that laugh for a moment. Then the laughter stopped, and there, in that busy canteen, Claire almost believed she saw love in the eyes of the surgeon.

The strobe lighting gave Claire a headache, and she began to realise that she wasn't enjoying the hospital disco. If only the music weren't so loud! Yet she knew the fault lay with herself: she was a senior staff nurse now and simply too old for this sort of gathering. The fact that she hadn't been too old for hospital 'hops' even a month ago was a fact she preferred to ignore.

'Having a good time, Claire?' That was Jill, whirling around with her boyfriemd, her face green in the reflected light, then turning orange. Then she was whisked away before Claire had time to shout out that she was having a great time. Someone who evidently was, though, was Katy Colby, Claire having persuaded her father to let her stay out late.

'A hospital disco?' John had said suspiciously, when, in the canteen, she had searched desperately for an innocuous subject. The brief glimpse of what she hoped was love had been all *too* brief, and she was certain now that she had been mistaken.

'Mmm, I'm sure Katy would enjoy it, and I'd see she got home safely. There's nothing for her to do in Hemsley Green and she'll get bored. The devil finds work for idle hands, as my dad used to say!'

'He was right,' John said drily. 'I'm supposed to be

giving Katy my undivided attention, but it hasn't worked out that way. Yes, by all means take her to the disco, but I'll see she gets home at a proper hour — there's no need for you to put yourself out.'

Despite Claire's protestations, John had been adamant: Claire could take Katy there and endeavour to keep an eye on her, but he would call for her at ten, leaving Claire to enjoy the rest of the evening.

Now it was nearly ten and, far from enjoying the evening, Claire was wishing she could return home with Katy's father! Yet one of her friends was expecting a lift to the other end of the village, and it was unlikely they would get away much before midnight. She supposed she had better remind Katy that Daddy would be here any minute. Woe betide the girl if she weren't ready!

Daddy was someone who had to be obeyed; that much had been evident from Katy's excited chatter on their way to the disco. It sounded as if Mummy had held her on too loose a rein and in consequence Katy now found Daddy's idea of what was right rather irksome. 'Ten o'clock! How can I bear to leave then?' she had complained as they neared the hall where the disco was being held.

'Your father wasn't keen on you going at all, but he must trust you or he would have refused,' Claire had said carefully. 'Twelve is a bit young for a hospital disco, and it's only because you're coming as my guest that you got a ticket. That, and the fact that Daddy is a consultant,' she'd added firmly, and Katy had subsided.

She was nowhere to be seen as Claire made her way to the cloakroom on the dot of ten. 'Oh, please don't keep Daddy waiting,' Claire muttered to herself. There was someone who would be blamed if she did, that was for sure!

He was waiting in the vestibule when at length she emerged, somewhat dishevelled, and without Katy. 'I suppose you've lost my daughter,' was all he said, but Claire flared up.

'She was here at a quarter to — I saw her! She was

with one of my friends, then she went to the cloakroom
and——' Claire ground to a halt, aware that she hadn't
made a very good job of being a chaperon. Yet she'd
had the girl under her eagle eye for most of the
evening, making sure she drank only squash and didn't
dance with anyone undesirable. As the disco was for
nurses and junior doctors, everyone knew who Katy
was, so there was no danger of her being prop-
ositioned—far from it!

'Don't worry, Claire—she'll turn up. It's one of
Katy's favourite tricks—set everyone's teeth on edge,
then appear as if nothing has happened. Enjoying the
disco?' There was laughter in John's voice, and Claire
relaxed.

'No, not really,' she admitted. 'It's so loud and—I
don't know, perhaps I'm tired.'

'All that housework you do when you're off duty, I
imagine. You're back tomorrow, I see,' he went on,
and Claire felt absurdly pleased that he had noticed
her name on the duty roster.

'Mmm, I'm on lates—two in a row because Sister's
going away,' she began, then wondered belatedly with
whom Sister was going away. John was off for the
same days as Stella Pountney. Not that it meant
anything, of course. Really, she was getting to be as
big a gossip as the juniors!

'Sister Pountney and I are going in opposite directions,' John said suddenly, and Claire didn't know
where to put her face. Then he laughed, displaying
even white teeth. 'Let the grapevine know, will you?
They seem to have us matched, and probably hatched
as well!'

'Hospitals run on gossip—you know that,' Claire
said defensively, secretly pleased none the less. 'Where
are you going?'

'To a computer conference in Newcastle. You ought
to learn about them, Claire. Look, why not come back
to the manor with Katy? I'll show you around my
temporary den, word processor and all.'

That sounded promising, but Claire had to explain

about her friend. 'She won't want to leave a minute before they close and I can't let her down.'

'If you're giving her a lift, your friend can't expect you to stay just to oblige her, not if it's such a disaster.' John winced as there was a sudden crash of drums. Then his expression changed, and Claire's eyes followed his gaze. Katy was responsible for the drumming! She was sitting up beside the small group which had been formed by the male nurses. Face flushed, eyes alight, she was staring defiantly at her father.

Oh, dear, trouble ahead, Claire thought. Then she began pushing her way through the throng of dancers, and held out her hand to Katy. 'Time to go, Katy!' she bellowed, wondering whether she would go deaf from the noise. 'Daddy's waiting.' After a second's hesitation, the girl got up, bestowed a beaming smile on the group then followed Claire, who didn't look back.

'One daughter, safe and sound, Mr Colby,' Claire said primly. 'I'll see you out then hang around for an hour or so, I think.'

'Yes, of course, Staff Nurse.' John's voice was equally formal. 'Had a good evening, poppet?' he asked Katy, who was scowling at them both.

'I wish I could stay longer, Daddy—couldn't I?' She hung on her father's arm, and he chuckled.

'Next time, certainly. You were ready on time tonight and that's a sign of a mature personality. Thank Staff Nurse for bringing you.'

'Thank you, Nurse.' Was there an edge to Katy's voice? It just needed her to suspect that a certain Staff Nurse Shaw fancied her father and Fireworks Day would come much earlier than usual!

Next morning, a weary Claire had almost decided on a lie-in, since she wasn't on duty until twelve-thirty. Then a glance out of the window changed her mind— summer was back!

'Up with the lark, Nurse,' she muttered, reaching for her caftan. A quick wash, some belated attention to the house-plants, which were beginning to take over the house, then a swim would be rather nice. She and

Suzanne had discussed having a small swimming-pool
in the garden and there was certainly room enough.
But with Suzanne away so much it hardly seemed
worth it, and Claire knew who would have the chore
of keeping it clean!

That was *one* chore she wasn't taking on. There was
a perfectly good pool at the hospital and that was
where she would go. She was still of the same mind as
she ate her breakfast toast a little later. Then the
phone went. It was John Colby. 'I'm not on duty until
two, so I've decided to spend the morning lotus-eating.
How about lunching wth me?'

Claire hesitated, wanting yet not wanting to accept.
'With you and Katy, do you mean?'

'No, just me. I thought it would be a thank-you for
taking care of her last night. We could discuss computers if you want a change from shop-talk,' he went
on, sounding annoyed.

'Yes, I'd like that. Thank you,' Claire said dully.
She didn't want a duty lunch. She longed to be invited
out because *he* wanted to spend time with her. 'Shall
we meet in town? That would be best, because I'm on
duty at twelve-thirty and I needn't come back home.
It will have to be a very quick lunch, I'm afraid.'

There was a heavy sigh at the other end. 'A sand-
wich and a cup of coffee, then. I'll see you.' The line
went dead, leaving Claire to stare at the receiver
before cradling it. John hadn't said what time he was
coming, or if he had accepted her suggestion that they
meet in town. The man was taking her for granted,
and she decided he was getting just like Martin
Medhurst. Well, he would have to wait because she
was definitely going to the swimming-pool first.

The solitary polka-dot plant she'd missed when
watering the others stared reproachfully at her as she
passed it in the hall half an hour later. Yes, she must
just see to that before going out. And it needed
repotting by the looks of it. Just a little water for now
then——

Then came a sharp ring on the bell followed by a
voice calling through the letterbox. Martin! Carefully

Claire inched the door open. 'Hello, you're an early bird—I was just going out.'

'You don't have to keep me on the doorstep—I'm not going to bite!' Martin sounded happy for once, the old Martin she remembered, and, believing he and his wife had made up, Claire let him in. 'Where are you off to?' He glanced at her jeans and T-shirt, his gaze lingering on her breasts, and Claire wished she had slipped on a cardigan. No, Martin would never change.

'I'm going to water one more plant, then I'm off to the hospital,' she said shortly. 'Oh, and close the door, will you? It's been a good year for wasps. Then there's been loads of ants, and we——' She wasn't allowed to finish, for Martin had taken her in his arms and he began to kiss her soundly.

For a second she responded. After all, it wasn't so long ago that she and Martin had been everything to each other. And hadn't she nearly died of a broken heart when he left? Yes, she was entitled to—— No! Belatedly wriggling free, an angry Claire faced him. 'That was rotten of you, Martin! What about Jacinth? You were telling me only a few days ago that you still missed her. You don't seem to be missing her *that* much! Or did you just feel in a randy mood and I'm a suitable substitute?'

Martin reddened. 'I'm sorry, Claire. Believe me, I didn't mean that to happen. But we did have some good times, and seeing you here, looking so seductive, I couldn't help myself. Am I forgiven?' His eyes met hers for once, and Claire nodded.

'Yes, OK. But it wasn't just good times with me—I actually *loved* you! How about that for a joke?' Tears weren't far away, so she turned aside, gazing fixedly at the polka-dot plant for a moment. 'I was just going to water you, wasn't I?' she muttered. 'You'd better go, Martin. Oh—have you seen. . .?' She ground to a halt. No, she could hardly ask him about John! 'What about your parents? I did ring them, you know, and Aunt Medhurst said she'd pop in but she hasn't.'

'Mother feels a bit guilty, Claire, I think that's it. She knew that you and I were. . . Well, anyway, that's in the past. But that wasn't what you started to say, was it? Have I seen a particular consultant surgeon, perhaps?'

Now it was Claire's turn to redden. 'John phoned me earlier, thanking me for taking Katy to the hospital disco. Have you seen her this morning?' Defiantly Claire met his glance. 'She was supposed to help me with the garden but it wouldn't be very interesting for her, I suppose.'

Martin shrugged. 'Weird sort of girl, isn't she? She certainly keeps tabs on her father, particularly when there's a pretty girl about! I suppose she hopes he and Tania will make it up.'

'Yes, I think she does. Perhaps they will — I hope so,' Claire said quietly, thinking of the children. It would be best for them, even if it wouldn't suit Staff Nurse Shaw.

'Do you?' Martin looked surprised. 'I rather thought you fancied John. No, he's a high-and-mighty consultant, isn't he?'

'And I'm only a lowly staff nurse! Anyway, I *am* going out, so. . .'

Instead of taking the hint, Martin produced a crumpled letter from his back pocket. 'Look, before you go, just read this through for me, will you? It's to Jacinth, and I rather ground to a halt with it. You're a woman, you can tell me what she'd like me to say.'

Aghast, Claire stared at the letter. 'Just put in it what *you* would want to hear if you were Jacinth! For heaven's sake, Martin! Tell her you love her, or. . .' Claire nibbled her lip. As she had never met Jacinth, she couldn't be sure how she would react. 'No, perhaps not. Tell her you'd like to come up and talk things over with her. Then take her out somewhere romantic — a candlelit dinner for two? No, perhaps not,' she said again, and heard Martin's exasperated sigh. 'I don't know Jacinth so how can I advise you? Just ask if you can come up and talk to her. It's up to her then.'

'Yes, all right, Claire. Thanks, anyway. It's just that you always knew the right words and I never did — that was the trouble, wasn't it?' Martin dropped a kiss on her brow, then, as Claire let him out, he patted her cheek. 'I'm a pest, aren't I? Thanks again—for everything.'

Glad that no one had seen him leave, Claire shut the door then leaned against it for a moment, her eyes closed, lost in memories. . . You could drown in memories, she'd read that somewhere. But Martin was in the past and no, she didn't actually want him back. Not now. In fact, the mature staff nurse wondered what the teenage Claire Shaw had seen in him! Perhaps they had both changed, yet some feeling remained, and he was obviously sorry for the hurt he'd caused her, as far as Martin would ever be sorry. The heartache she was feeling must be a hangover from that dreadful disco, to go with the headache which had tormented her all night.

'Oh, John,' she said aloud. 'If only. . .' Then, pulling herself together, she at last watered the waiting plant, and was just picking up her car keys when the bell rang. Hoping it wasn't Martin again, she opened the door, to find an unsmiling John Colby. Although she had no reason to feel guilty, she blushed, wondering if he had X-ray eyes like Sister Whitelaw and could actually see into her heart!

'I passed Martin on the way—he's an early bird, isn't he?' John's gaze was keen.

'He always was,' Claire said shortly. 'The early bird catches the worm, or so I'm told. Do you want to come in, or are we lunching extra early?'

'Sorry, I sound like a parent, don't I?' Unexpectedly, John smiled down at her, a smile of genuine warmth, to which Claire couldn't help but respond.

'That's natural, I suppose. Come in, though I was thinking of going over to the hospital and taking a dip in their pool. Martin kept me talking and I've gone off the idea now.' Claire yawned, thinking wistfully of her bed. Perhaps she should have had another hour.

'Gram's doing my round this morning and I'm walking the wards for him this evening, so I brought a mini-picnic since there isn't time for a proper lunch.' John indicated the plastic carrier. 'It's nothing very grand, but I sweet-talked Mrs Taylor!' He stood looking at her with an enigmatic smile on his face, and Claire rather wished he wouldn't stand so near, because yearning swept over her, a far different feeling from the one she'd had in Martin's arms. It wasn't fair!

'Thank you, but. . . I don't think so. I don't know what I want, to be perfectly honest.' From somewhere, Claire summoned up a smile, her huge eyes pleading with him for understanding, for compassion. He, above all people, must know how she felt.

'Claire, don't! Please.' John sounded — and looked — agonised, and Claire's gaze faltered.

'I haven't done anything so I don't know what it is I mustn't do!' She tried to make a joke of it, but the air was heavy with unspoken hopes, desires, and her voice died away.

'I hope. . .' he began, blue eyes intense as they rested on her face. 'Martin looked like the cat who'd been at the cream when I saw him. Claire — don't get involved.'

Claire gasped, but before she could tell him to mind his own business he put his hands on her shoulders, the warmth seeping into her flesh through the thin shirt, and she forgot what she had been about to say.

'Don't try to come between Martin and his wife — please. I know what it's like, trying to hang on to a relationship then finding out that you're the only one who cared, the only one who wanted to make a go of it, give it another chance.' Abruptly he moved his hands, gently caressing her arms, and Claire's heart did a quick loop-the-loop before gradually settling down.

Her lips parted, and she was about to tell him exactly what she thought of his remark, but she found herself swaying towards him instead, and their lips met in a kiss of such fierceness, such passion that she could hardly breathe.

'Oh, Claire.' John's lips left hers for a moment while he brushed them against her fragrantly scented hair. 'Claire, don't. . .' But she stood on tiptoe and wound her arms about his neck, and there was no more need for words.

After a moment that seemed to last for eternity they drew apart, but for Claire that was difficult to do. She wanted to remain in his arms, longed for more than a mere kiss, but there was Katy and his sons. . . Katy, who longed for her parents to be together again. Katy who might have been a younger version of herself, someone who had spent countless hours longing for a real family, a mother who was always there, a father who had time for her. . .

She drew a deep, shuddering breath, then licked her lips, John's eyes following the movement. 'You'd better go—I might get used to having you around!' she quipped, trying to hide her heartache behind a cheery smile, as ever.

'Do you want me to go? Claire, look at me,' he commanded, but she turned away, wiping her damp face with the back of her hand. Why it should be damp she couldn't think.

'You've got no right to lecture me about Martin.' Her voice was low, strained. 'What about you and Stella Pountney? You say you want your ex-wife back, that you care for her. Yet you carry on with other women at the hospital!' Her voice rose as indignation took over from heartache.

'Do I?' John sounded astonished. 'I'm not "carrying on", as you put it, with Stella! Good lord. . .' His voice trailed away, then he began to chuckle. 'She's an interesting companion, believe it or not, but if she's got the wrong idea that's her problem.'

'You're just as arrogant as Martin!' Claire snapped. 'He thinks all he has to do is come here with a sob story and I'll fall into his arms like. . .like a ripe fruit!'

'What sort of fruit would that be, I wonder?' he said musingly. 'An apple, perhaps? No, definitely a peach! A particularly delightful sweet peach, Claire.'

'Don't change the subject,' she said. 'You know what I mean. Sister Pountney actually *cares* for you!'

'Stella cares for the kudos of having a tame consultant around, perhaps, but not for me personally. Don't waste any tears on her. What's this about wanting my ex-wife back, anyway?'

Claire hesitated before replying. It was Katy who longed for Daddy and Mummy to be together, but she could hardly betray the girl's confidence. 'You said you wanted to hang on to your relationship and that you were the only one who cared. I've worked out for myself that Miss Wallace is your ex-wife, so. . .' Claire shrugged, as if saying the whole subject was a complete bore to her.

John stared down at the picnic he'd spread over the kitchen table, and Claire's eyes followed his. There were sandwiches, an appetising-looking salad, cold chicken, one of Mrs Taylor's home-made cakes, and fruit—the delightfully sweet peaches to which John had likened her only moments before. 'That was then, Claire, this is now,' he began. 'Tania and I were never compatible, and she had the wit to see it, I didn't. Now. . .' he spread his hands in a helpless gesture '. . .Katy would like to see us remarry. She makes no secret of that, but I——'

'What about the boys? You don't seem to be considering them,' Claire said sharply. 'It's always what Katy wants, but what about Robert and Johnnie? What do *they* feel?'

He looked blank. 'Who? Oh, the boys! They aren't old enough to really care one way or the other. They——'

'They're old enough to be consulted!' Claire broke in. 'Boys *need* a father, John. They ought to be living with you. I was only eight when my mother died, but I still remember her, still feel the hurt that she should go away and leave me. My father thought I was too young to understand, but I wasn't!'

He looked shaken, and Claire almost regretted her harsh words. 'Oh, Claire, I can't bear to see you hurt! Look, let me explain about the boys. They——'

'I don't want to hear any more about *any* of your children, Mr Colby, thank you very much. What Martin and I share is our business, not yours or anyone else's.' With an effort, Claire kept her voice cold, disdainful. Let him think what he liked; she didn't care.

'I was going to explain about the boys, but perhaps it's as well you don't know,' John said heavily, turning to stare out of the window. 'Katy was right,' he went on, without telling her what it was that Katy was right about. He swung round to face her, and Claire, who had, a moment before, been staring with longing at his back, now schooled herself to keep her gaze neutral. Sufficiently so, she hoped.

'You're doing a great job on Westfield, Claire — I can sense a different atmosphere there already! Keep up the good work. I——' He shrugged, a weary gesture. 'We'd better take a rain-check on that meal. You can enjoy the picnic by yourself. Perhaps one day when you're off duty we can have a proper meal. . . Katy might like to join us.'

'And the boys,' Claire said stonily, and a faint smile flitted across the handsome face opposite her.

'Yes, why not the boys? They don't get many treats, do they? Take care, little one.'

Claire stood silently as if turned to stone as John let himself out. Then she flew to the hall window, where she could follow him with her eyes. Yes, there he was. He looked. . . She frowned. He looked as if he'd been kicked, beaten down by some great sorrow.

Before she could think better of it, she ran to the door, about to call after him, beg him to stay so that she could soothe away his sorrows. Yes, and if he wanted her she would do far more than that. Why should they deny themselves? Katy and the boys need never know, need never be aware that consultant and staff nurse were lovers. They could——

Then the telephone rang, and Claire went automatically to answer it, but her thoughts went winging silently after the man she loved.

CHAPTER NINE

THE ambulance was probably giving Wendy a bumpy ride, Claire mused as she followed it in her car. The lane near Wendy's house fully lived up to the folklore about ancient Sussex roads, and must have been difficult for the driver to negotiate. At last, though, they were on the main road leading out of Hemsley Green, and would be in Elmleigh within minutes.

How glad she was now that she had answered the telephone! If the call had come even a few minutes later, she and John might have been locked in a passionate embrace, lost to the world and perhaps not even *hearing* the telephone. Saved by the bell with a vengeance, Claire thought grimly as she changed down, mentally reviewing the events.

The call had come from Wendy's neighbour, saying that Wendy's sickness and lack of appetite had suddenly worsened, and that she was in 'fearful pain'. The pain had proved to be minor and was possibly indigestion, but Wendy was definitely dehydrated, and Claire had called the GP, thanking her stars that she was a local doctor's daughter—it opened doors as if by magic. Now the ambulance slowed as it approached the hospital drive, and Claire glanced at her watch. She would have time to see Wendy settled into Camber before dashing off to the locker-room to change for duty. The proposed morning's swim already seemed a distant memory. So did John's kiss.

Although she hurried to Westfield, she was nearly five minutes late, and Sister Pountney eyed her grimly. 'Sorry, Sister! One of my neighbours had an emergency and she's on Camber now.' Claire settled into the chair the junior had hastily vacated, and got out her notebook and pen, determine not to be cowed.

'Emergencies come upon us when we least expect them,' Sister said dourly. 'We had one last night and another this morning.' She sighed. 'I suppose I had better start the handover again, so pay attention, Staff Nurse!'

Since this was Claire's first day back, there was plenty to catch up on even without the emergencies, and her notebook was soon filling up with diagnoses, prognoses, details of operations and medication prescribed.

'And with Mr Colby going off to a conference, Gram and Mr O'Brien's firm are going to have to cope,' Stella Pountney finished with another sigh, as though it was all getting too much for her. And perhaps it was, Claire mused, as she made her way to the ward to speak to each patient.

'Metal fatigue, I expect!' Nurse Fryer whispered to her as they fell into step. 'That computer she calls a heart is in need of a good mechanic. She hasn't been herself since I found her and John arguing yesterday morning — you should have seen them!'

'Were they?' Claire asked, startled. 'Not actually having a row on the ward?'

'Well, no,' the other staff nurse admitted, 'not a row exactly — more a full and frank exchange of opinions, as politicians call it! Basically it's been an awful three days!'

One of the emergencies had been a collapse on the ward, or, more correctly, in the corridor just outside Westfield. This wasn't a patient but a visitor, an old friend who had come to see George Upshall. He was now in ITU, and Claire could well imagine how that episode had set George back.

The previous evening's emergency had come to them via A and E and Theatre. Alan Keates had been involved in an RTA on the corner by the hospital, a noted accident blackspot, and had to undergo surgery, a splenectomy, straight from A and E. He was young and apparently in good physical shape otherwise, Claire noted as she reached his bed, though he had suffered cracked ribs and severe bruising in the accident.

Smiling down at him, she said, 'Hello, Mr Keates,

I'm Claire Shaw, the staff nurse. How are you feeling now? Any pain?'

Alan made an attempt at a grin, then pursed his swollen lips in a soundless whistle. 'Thought I'd died and gone up to heaven! If I'd known nurses were all so young and luscious, I'd have ruptured my spleen before!'

Claire chuckled, then reached for his chart. So far, so good, she noted. 'You were lucky to get off so lightly, though it doesn't seem lightly, I know. Your girlfriend phoned during the handover — she's coming in after work.'

The patient moved restlessly, his grin fading. There was a tautness about his mouth that suggested pain even though he denied feeling any. 'I don't want to see Shirley, Nurse. I don't want her to see *me*! She'll faint,' he mumbled, then closed his eyes.

He certainly wasn't a pretty sight, with a redivac drainage bottle leading from his wound, a naso-gastric tube strapped to his cheek, and an IV running, but surely Shirley would put *his* needs first? There was nothing to cause a fainting fit, Claire mused, but such sights were alarming to the lay person and she would look out for the girl later on, try to prepare her. In the meantime, Alan's pain must be dealt with, and a nurse must somehow be found to keep a special eye on him.

Two patients had been discharged but the beds had rapidly filled up and now the ward was full again, she noted as she gradually worked her way through the cubicles, being greeted by varying degrees of cheerfulness, and a number of wolf-whistles!

'Now, now, boys, you can't have missed me that much!' she said later, as she went round with the medicine trolley. 'How are you, George?' she asked as she reached George Upshall's bed. He was sitting beside his bed struggling to complete a crossword. Though still a sick man, he was making a better recovery than they had dared hope.

'I'll do, as your Mr Colby says. Heard about old Harry, did you? Fell like a log, he did, right out there.' George pointed to a spot just in front of the patients' lavatories. 'I thought he was a goner and no mistake! Then that sister came bustling up and got them doctors organised. I'll say this for her, she knows her stuff.'

Claire solemnly agreed that this was so. 'I haven't heard from ITU about your friend, and no news is good news, George. I'll send a nurse down to them when the ward's quiet to see how things are, so don't worry too much,' she smiled. 'We don't like to ring them if it can be avoided, not when they're so busy.' And so full that they couldn't cope with any more patients, she added silently, recalling that she must also find time to pop along to Camber to see Wendy. But time just flew by, and it was her supper-break before she could do so.

It seemed to her that all the patients and their relatives had saved up their queries while she was on days off, and had decided to present them to her on one evening! Alan Keates's girlfriend hadn't yet put in an appearance, she noted as she walked briskly along to Camber. That would be another problem for later. As it was, she wouldn't get any supper — seeing Wendy was more important.

Wendy was resting, staring straight ahead. An IV drip had been set up to get some fluid into her dehydrated body, and she seemed comfortable, the earlier pain having passed off. 'That nice surgeon says he's a-coming to sort me out tomorrer,' Wendy informed her. 'I ain't had no visitors yet, but Next-Door says she'll pop along when she can.'

'What about Sam? Shall I ring over and ask if he can come in?'

'No, don't bother him tonight. See him when I see him, I expect. One of the girls'll be in tomorrer.' She didn't sound very enthusiastic, but Claire refrained from passing comment. Having checked the admission notes in the ward office, she knew that a possible malignancy had been suggested by John, though nothing had been palpable on physical examination. Wendy had been sent down for straight X-rays but for now John wanted her to rest and taken in fluids, which he considered more important than anything else at present.

On her way back to Westfield, Claire was hailed rather hesitantly by David Dunster. Surprised, she stopped, automatically adjusting her cap as she so often did when she was ill at ease. After all, Mr Dunster had seen her in the arms of a certain consultant!

Of course he didn't refer to that occasion, but it was still fresh in Claire's mind as they spoke. 'Surely your gran isn't back?'

Smilingly, he shook his head. 'No, not Gran. She's fine, thanks. One of our neighbours is in the ENT ward and I promised I'd look in on her. Gran wanted me to, so. . .' He laughed, also feeling uneasy, Claire suspected.

'I won't keep you, then, Mr Dunster. It's been nice seeing you again,' she said brightly, then made as if to return to her ward, but he laid a hand on her arm, then quickly snatched it away, perhaps mindful of people passing in the corridor.

'Look, I know you're busy, and you've probably got a full social life, but I wondered — for Gran's sake, really — if I could treat you to a meal one day. Lunch, perhaps. Gran would like that,' he hurried on, going rather pink, and Claire felt sorry for him.

'Yes, that would be lovely. I'm on late again tomorrow, though — perhaps one day next week? Oh, but you'll be working!' That would be an escape clause, Claire thought, but her hopes were dashed: Mr Dunster worked flexitime and could take an extended lunch-break. When she told him that *she* couldn't, he looked so dejected that she felt mean, so a date was made for the following Friday, when Claire knew she would be on earlies, though that left little enough time for a proper meal. Never mind, she thought, as she hurried by, ye olde Horse and Crown would have her custom yet again!

It was too much to hope that she could avoid John, since he was working all evening, and about half-past seven he appeared on Westfield. Claire, having dele-

gated the report writing to one of the juniors as good
practice, was about to make a round of the patients.
'Just put down what you've seen and any observations
that have been made on each patient. Oh, and don't
forget to mention any patients who seem restless
or——'

'Worried. Quite right, Staff Nurse,' a voice put in,
and Claire looked up from the desk where she had
been giving final instructions to the student. Her hands
strayed automatically to her cap, then she turned the
gesture into a brushing-back of a strand of hair instead.
There was no need to feel uncomfortable in John's
presence; after all, *he* couldn't know she had been
about to invite him into her bed!

'Were you wanting to do a round, Mr Colby?' she
asked crisply, mindful of the junior's alert expression
and waving antennae.

'That's why I'm here,' was the cool response, and a
chastened Claire led the way to Alan Keates's bed.

It was Gram who had operated on Alan, and the
consultant spent some time at his bed. 'I've got a hell
of a lot of aches and pains, Doc,' Alan said, with an
attempt at a grin, and Claire smiled at him, wondering
if he was upset that Shirley hadn't called in, after all.

'You were lucky to come out of that accident alive,'
John said bluntly. 'And lucky my registrar decided you
probably had a delayed splenic rupture. Sometimes
the signs and symptoms disappear, only to come back
with a vengeance, perhaps days later.' Having
reassured the patient that he would be able to live
perfectly well without his spleen, they passed on to
George Upshall. Thankfully, his friend was still
recovering after his myocardial infarction, though he
was overweight and not the fittest of men, but John
managed to reassure George without going into too
many details.

'Never lie to the patient but avoid telling the truth,'
the surgeon said as they walked on to the next cubicle.
'Isn't that the procedure here? Have you had any more
ideas about improving patient-care at the District?' he
asked unexpectedly, and Claire hesitated.

'I think relatives should be involved more, and not treated as a nuisance at best, or as simpletons at worst,' she said tartly. 'What about your patient-teaching sessions? Are you getting on with your research or have you come to a dead end?' she countered, and a low chuckle broke from him.

'Ah, them Upstairs, you mean? Yes, they're a load of conservative die-hards, aren't they? If it's been good enough for their predecessors, then don't change it. That seems to be their policy,' he sighed, then chuckled again. 'Never mind, if something — or some-one — is easily won, it spoils the fun.' His eyes met hers, that mocking expression back again.

Now what did he mean by *that* remark? Claire wondered later, as she prepared to go off duty. The ward lights had been dimmed, the report given, and there was no earthly reason why she shouldn't go home to her bed, yet. . . Yet she still had the urge to invite John Colby back to share that bed. She could well imagine what Upstairs would make of that!

Feeling that John had been serious when he had asked for a list of possible improvements, Claire duly wrote out a few suggestions the following day and took them on duty with her. Then she remembered — wasn't he going off to his computer conference this afternoon? She was surprised, therefore, to meet him as she arrived in the surgical unit. But of course — it was the monthly meeting of Upstairs, and John would have had to attend. All the seniors attended unless they were actually in the middle of an operation! The custom of the house, Claire thought drily, as she murmured, 'Good afternoon, sir.'

'Is it? Tell me just *one* thing that's good about it and I'll stand you a champagne supper,' he said softly, and Claire laughed.

'Upstairs have been snapping at your heels — I recognise the signs,' she said primly, and was rewarded by a smile. 'I brought you a list of what *I* would like changed here, but you're wasting your time, you know.'

He took the list from her, their fingers just touching, and Claire schooled herself not to pull her hand away. Really, she felt as if she'd been burnt! He was far too attractive for his own good. But, Staff Nurse, remember Martin Medhurst. Ah, yes, Martin. . .

'Something on that brilliant mind of yours?' John asked, a glint of humour in his eyes. 'Martin, perhaps?' His gaze was perceptive. 'I heard him on the phone to you this morning. He sounded wildly excited—hasn't won a football pool, has he?'

Claire shook her head, tempted to tell him but deciding against it. 'He doesn't need to win the pools, he's got plenty of money. He's going back to Suffolk after the weekend—I expect you knew that?'

'Yes, so he said. He's planning to spend next weekend with someone—I hope it isn't you, Claire.'

Claire only just remembered to keep her voice down. 'You have a nerve! I told you, my private life is no business of yours! I——' She had been about to say, I wish it were, but was able to bite the words back in time. *He* had one ex-wife, one ward sister, and yes, one third-year student, for hadn't she seen him in Elmleigh with Student Nurse Wise? They had obviously had elevenses together, for they'd been coming out of the teashop in the High Street. Then he must have gone straight to the meeting with Upstairs. Hadn't he done *any* work this morning?

'Have you seen Wendy this morning?' she went on. 'I've come in a bit early so I can pop in to see her—she didn't look well last night.'

The abrupt change of subject seemed to startle John, and his eyes narrowed. 'I can't see the connection but yes, I came in early and I've seen *all* my patients, Staff Nurse Shaw. I'm not happy about Wendy, but it's probably her bowels—or bowel.'

'A malignancy, you think?'

'You know I can't say that, not without further tests—and she seems to have had enough tests each time she's been in. Don't let it get you down—you can't carry everyone's burdens, my dear.'

The endearment, slight though it was, caught Claire

by surprise, and she could feel herself colour, watched with evident interest by the surgeon. 'I don't try to!' she said, more sharply than she had intended.

'You look adorable when you blush,' he observed, thus causing more of a blush than ever, and Claire scowled at him, his laughter following her along the corridor.

'Mr Colby did a round then made notes for his book,' the morning staff nurse told her at the hand-over, 'but then we had a transfer from medical — a peptic ulcer. He's been on Mayfield Ward with hae-morrhage from the ulcer and Mr Colby offered to take him for obs now the bleeding's settled — query possible surgery as it's a long-standing case. And he's been moaning ever since he arrived!'

'Has the peptic ulcer a name?' Claire asked quietly. 'And *why* is he moaning?'

'He's a Mr Elliott, aged. . .' The staff nurse searched among her notes. 'Yes, aged fifty-one. He's quieter now, and no, he isn't in pain — it isn't that sort of moaning! He's a complainer,' Claire's opposite number said tartly. 'He used to have private health insurance but he couldn't afford to keep it up, so he's back to the good old NHS! He says none of us has any sympathy with him. They expect miracles sometimes,' she grumbled.

'All the time,' Claire said lightly. 'Where have you put him? Surely we hadn't a vacancy? Mr Renton is due——'

Number Seven said we could move Mr Renton to Camber's side-room just for the one night, so our new friend is in George Upshall's bay. Have a pleasant afternoon!'

Claire's heart sank. It sounded like a troublesome day, and how she was to get through three days without the often arrogant but always adorable John Colby she did not know. And what *was* he doing in the town with Nurse Wise?

Claire frowned as she surveyed the contents of the linen cupboard two days later. Staff Nurse Rees had warned her that stocks were getting low and that requests for extra linen were being ignored, but this was ridiculous. Two beds at least had draw-sheets which were patched, and one, which Claire had indignantly discarded, had a big hole in it. Make do and mend, with a vengeance! Well, something must be done and——

'Haven't come into the cupboard to cry, have you, Nurse?' a voice hissed in her ear, and Claire turned sharply, almost colliding with the athletic frame of one consultant surgeon. 'Isn't this the time-honoured place for nurses to weep into their aprons, after Sister or Staff Nurse has been horrid to them?' John went on, his body effectively blocking Claire's escape route.

'What are you doing here? And no, I haven't come in to cry, because I've been horrid to myself! Don't forget, I'm Acting Sister today. And you're in my way,' Claire rushed on, that tell-tale blush letting her down. He really had a most unsettling effect on her, and the sooner summer ended the better!

'Your face clouded over then, Claire—it was like the sun going in,' John said softly, putting out a hand and tenderly tucking in a strand of bright hair which was threatening to escape from her cap.

Claire tensed, willing him to go away. 'I was thinking nasty thoughs about the bed-linen situation,' she prevaricated, and he raised a brow, a mocking gleam in his eyes.

'Fascinating subject, bed-linen,' he murmured. 'Let's discuss it, shall we, Acting Sister? How about seductively satin sheets and lace-edged pillows? What colour would you like?'

Yes, he was definitely mocking her! Claire moistened her dry lips. 'I don't think the patients would appreciate satin sheets *or* lace-edged pillows. Nor would the nurses who have to change wet beds! And now, *if* you will excuse me, I have to report the lack of linen,' she said sternly. 'Heads will roll!'

He chuckled. 'I'll let you go on payment of a forfeit, Acting Sister Shaw—one kiss.' With that, he gently pinioned her arms at her sides, and since Claire was already pressed against the shelves there was no escape.

The forfeit duly paid, the surgeon's lips left hers and trailed a row of seductive little kisses along her cheeks then her earlobe, which he proceeded to nibble gently, while Claire, caught in his arms, really couldn't evade him. Not that she tried all that hard, she had to admit to herself. 'Stop it! You mustn't — you've no right!' she said at last.

'Mmm? What was that, Acting Sister? I didn't quite catch that remark. Tell me again,' he demanded, then effectively prevented her from doing so by pressing his lips against hers again.

'You haven't the right!' Claire said, when at length he let her speak. 'What about Katy and the boys? And there's Nurse Wise!'

John let her go, but their bodies were still close together, and she could feel his warm breath on her cheek. 'Nurse Wise?' he said blankly, and Claire nodded, then hastily adjusted her cap before pushing him firmly away.

'Don't pretend you don't know who I mean! You had elevenses with her the other morning,' she said rashly, and he chuckled.

'Did I? You mean Natalie? Her husband's in computers and they've both been offering their advice.' Laugher was in his eyes as he gazed down at Claire with what might have been love, if the idea hadn't been so preposterous.

Claire, not knowing what to say and feeling foolish, tried to shrug as if the whole matter weren't of the slightest interest to her. In the confined space, she merely succeeded in moving even nearer to him, her breasts brushing against his arms. She heard his sharp intake of breath, then he moved aside. 'Perhaps I'd better go, Acting Sister — I don't want to distract you,' he said softly.

'Perhaps you had. Oh, what happened to Newcastle and computers? You aren't on duty, are you?' John was wearing casual clothes and no tie, but fortunately he was wearing a shirt!

'It was literally a flying visit. I couldn't spare the time for the whole conference, though it *was* on my off-duty. Research beckoned and there's a patient I particularly wanted to interview, then Upstairs rang me — the unit's been busy, by the sound of it,' he went on, moving to the door of the walk-in cupboard.

'Yes, it has — that coach crash has taken all the beds. We had one of them, but Hastings Ward had to take the overflow.' Elmleigh was a popular holiday resort, and two coaches had collided just outside the town, killing one of the drivers and injuring several passengers. 'Your Mr Elliott's been sent home with an outpatients appointment, by the way. Upstairs said we couldn't keep him. Camber's had to put up extra beds, and. . . Oh — have you seen Wendy?' Claire went on.

'No, I'm going to look in on there when I've finished Westfield. Officially I'm not here, but Gram's got an emergency. It's a pity about Mr Elliott — he was my guinea-pig, but he'll be back shortly for surgery.'

'Guinea-pig?' Claire said bleakly. 'Do you mean you had him transferred from Mayfield just for your research?'

'They needed his bed and we had a vacancy, so yes, I thought he would be useful for my textbook. Why? He needed the opportunity to talk — no one on Medical had time for him!' John's voice had an edge to it, but so did Claire's as she told him what she thought of such an attitude.

'That's because on Medical it's one solid grind — bedpans, backs, TPR. . .' Claire counted them off on her fingers. '*We* hadn't time for him either, not after that crash. We're short-staffed at the best of times, and *you* decide we have to go through all the rigmarole of preparing a bed, settling him in, doing obs, just so you can fill up a few pages of your textbook! And how do you think Mr Elliott felt?'

'Ah, I wondered when we would get to the patient's feelings, Staff Nurse,' John said grimly, while Claire eyed him resentfully. 'We're here for the patients, and yes, I *do* know how Mr Elliott felt because I asked for his co-operation. Since he's had several admissions he was anxious to make his views known!'

'He made them known to the nurses all right,' Claire said feelingly, some of her anger subsiding now that she knew the patient hadn't been just a pawn. 'He had one of the juniors in tears and *I* had to spend precious time trying to persuade her not to discontinue her training!'

'If she's going to be upset that easily, perhaps she would be better working in an office!' he flashed back. 'Mr Elliott found better understanding of his needs on Westfield than anywhere else he's been warded, and he had particular praise for Staff Nurse Shaw,' he went on relentlessly. 'I'm sorry your nurses had extra work, but it won't hurt them, and I would have discharged him today, in any case. He *could* have had another haemorrhage, though — don't let his label of "difficult patient" blind you to that fact.' He paused, then gave a bleak smile. 'You look so luscious when you're angry that it's a wonder I can keep my hands off you,' he said unexpectedly.

'You couldn't keep them off just now!' she said pertly. 'But you needn't try to change the subject — it seems to me that anything goes just so long as it aids your research. People don't matter; they're just a means to an end.' Claire knew she was being unfair, that John was a deeply caring man, but surgeons had to remain aloof to some extent, and perhaps he didn't realise he used people. Well, someone ought to tell him, and it might as well be her! 'You use people, John. You may not realise it, but you do, even patients.'

He looked stunned, then gave a wry smile. 'You sound like Tania, and you may both be right. And while I'm using people, how about coming to London with me when I finish here? Katy has to learn that she can't have everything she wants just by wishing. No amount of wishing would tempt Tania to have me back, I can assure you!' he went on, grimly. '*We* could make a home together. You could continue in surgical, broaden your horizons a bit — perhaps go on a course.

I was going to Canada, but that's been cancelled now so I'll have to look around, and London's where it's all happening. I don't intend to stay buried in Elmleigh for the rest of my life!'

'How about coming to London with me. . .? *We* could make a home together'. Oh, how tempting that was! But Claire resolutely shook her head. Suzanne's words came back to her: married men were all past and no future. Substitute 'divorced' for 'married' and you had one consultant surgeon. Yet a home with John Colby. . . Hadn't she yearned for just that? But she had yearned for *marriage* with John. She didn't want another shabby affair, another year or two of being taken for granted then pushed aside when someone more exciting turned up.

Hurt beyond measure because he hadn't mentioned love, let alone marriage, she said, 'I'm sorry, but you're taking too much for granted. Anyway, Martin wouldn't like it,' she added, then wished the words unsaid as John's face hardened. Why on earth did she have to say that?

'I was forgetting Martin — where are you going for the weekend?'

Claire hesitated. Actually, she was on duty all Saturday, with only Sunday free, but wasn't about to tell him. 'I don't know, but we'll find somewhere. Give my love to Katy and the boys, won't you?' she said sweetly, even though her heart was breaking. Two men in her life and neither of them wanted to marry her! She was good enough for sex but not for marriage, a lifelong commitment, and that was what really hurt.

'Yes, of course I will,' John was saying. 'We're spending part of Sunday with Tania, but I'll be working most of the weekend, if you should find you need me,' he said meaningfully, then stalked away, leaving Claire to clutch a draw-sheet to her chest and wish it were the consultant surgeon.

Despite her anger with him, Claire couldn't help feeling glad he was back. Now she could relax her vigilance a little — the boss was back to ease her burdens!

These included a patient with a peptic ulcer which had perforated. Gram had operated that morning, and now Mr Smith was back in the ward, his wife sitting with him. He was on a drip and automatically Claire checked it on passing. 'Everything all right, Mrs Smith?' she whispered, as the patient's eyes were closed.

'Yes, thanks, Nurse. He seems OK.' Mrs Smith nodded towards her husband. 'But I'm worried about our girl. I've left her with a sitter but she can't stay all night, and I really ought to get back.' She shook her head sadly. 'If it's not one thing it's another.'

'You can come to the office and talk to me, if you like,' Claire offered. 'Your husband doesn't need you all the time, you know. Let him sleep, if he can.' He would probably need more analgesia before long, Claire judged, but didn't tell his wife that as she led the way towards the office. She did wonder whether he had closed his eyes because he wanted to be alone, as she had noted that every so often his wife would lean over him and listen, as if half expecting him to expire any moment. That kind of worry rapidly communicated itself.

Mrs Smith refused an offer of tea. 'I've had two cups already, thanks all the same. He will be all right, won't he? He looked that ill and he's been cold and clammy and—oh, I don't know.' She buried her head in her hands, and Claire let her cry for a few moments. A good cry was worth a thousand words.

Then the words came: they had money problems and hadn't been able to pay the latest instalment on their credit cards. Then their gas fire had been condemned as dangerous, their daughter was developing school phobia, and, to cap it all, they would have to take in her disabled father because her elder sister had been taken to the psychiatric unit suffering from overwork and complete nervous exhaustion.

'She's always cared for him! It isn't fair that I've got to take him in—not when Steve's so ill.' Mrs Smith's face was full of angry resentment, but Claire couldn't help feeling sorry for the other daughter who had presumably been left to cope alone with a difficult parent.

'I'll ask the social worker to contact you.' Claire glanced at her watch. No, early evening was hardly the time for that. 'I'll ring her as soon as she comes on duty in the morning, and she'll be able to advise. You need to write to the credit-card companies, though — explain about your problems. Oh, what about your mortgage?'

That, too, was posing a problem, and must be worrying the patient as well as his wife, Claire reflected later, after she had seen Mrs Smith off the premises, reassured her that advice would be given as soon as possible, and that her husband was in good hands.

Then she went back to Steve Smith, to find that he was fully awake. Expressionless black eyes gazed back at her and there was a half-smile on his lips. 'She goes on a bit, doesn't she? Expecting me to peg out any minute, I suppose,' Mr Smith went on, the little smile fading as he shifted his position, or tried to.

'Here, let me.' Mr Smith was propped up in bed now that his blood-pressure had reached a 'safe' settled level, and Claire carefully adjusted his back-rest and pillows. 'Is that easier?'

'Yes, thanks, Nurse. God, I could do with a smoke!'

'That's out of the question,' Claire said crisply. 'You've been very ill, you know,' she went on. 'You were in shock — that's why your wife is so concerned now, but Mr Colby is pleased with your progress.'

'Oh, good,' Mr Smith said sourly. 'My mouth's dry, and what about all these tubes and bottles? If that bloke's so "pleased with my progress", why hasn't he taken them out?' He was becoming fretful, impatient because events seemed to be moving too slowly for him, keen to be up and back to work, Claire thought as she detailed a nurse to take him the 'lollipop' type of mouthwash to suck. A typical ulcer personality, their Mr Smith. Despite Claire's assurance that he was going on well, and would be sitting out of bed in the morning, he was still impatient. Poor Mrs Smith!

Having heard enough of people's problems, Claire

popped in to see Sister Whitelaw for a few minutes.
'All ready for the off, Sister? I can't believe it's your
last week,' she said brightly, wishing that the retirement could be postponed. The District wouldn't be
the same without the sister's tart comments and smiling
face.

'Upstairs are making some kind of presentation.
Since we haven't generally seen eye to eye, I suppose
that's generous of them,' Sister said with a grim smile.

'You've *never* seen eye to eye with them, you mean,'
Claire said. 'Are you having a party?' she asked
casually, but Sister shook her head, the permed curls
dancing beneath the lace cap.

'No, I thought about bringing in a few bottles and
perhaps making a bit of a do, but Upstairs said not to.
They're going to lay on tea and sandwiches in the
canteen, apparently. But I'll have my special nurses
round to the bungalow once I've come to terms with
retirement. Then we'll have "a bit of a do"! You're
one of my special nurses,' Sister Whitelaw added, and
Claire smilingly tugged her forelock.

Sister evidently didn't know about the party they
had planned, and Upstairs, for once, hadn't put their
foot in it. 'Thank you, Sister. I'd like to see you at
home, presiding over the giant teapot you keep just
for visitors! Oh — what about Wendy Clark? Have you
seen the results of the barium meal?'

Although Sister assured her she hadn't and was
waiting for John to see them first, Claire rather thought
they weren't promising. Poor Wendy, now with so
much to live for. She ——

'Unhappy thoughts, Claire?' a coldly distant voice
enquired, and Claire glanced up, surprised to find that
she had found her way back to Westfield, and that
John was sitting in the office.

'Mmm, about Wendy — what did they find? Sister
wouldn't say.' Claire fixed her eyes on John, who
shook his head.

'She had a barium enema last admission, I see. My
predecessor seems to have been obsessed with bowels!'
he said sharply. 'It's gastric as I suspected, and I'm

operating tomorrow, see what I can do. Now, what about the patients on *this* ward?'

Claire knew he was quite right to pull her up. She was Westfield now, and it helped no one if half her mind was on Camber's patients. She took him through the Kardex, trying to bring him up to date, then came to Stephen Smith. 'He's in discomfort but refusing further analgesia. All he's asking for is a bit of peace and quiet,' Claire said. 'He doesn't want his wife visiting.' She went on to outline the family's financial difficulties. 'I think she makes him more anxious than he would be if left alone,' she ventured, and John nodded. 'Anyway, I'll fix up with the social workers to see her, try to set her own mind at ease. Alan Keates. . .' She hesitated. 'Comfortable but he's just broken with his girlfriend and he's feeling low. That's it, I think.' She flipped back the Kardex, then noticed John's eyes on the blank VDU in the corner.

'We really ought to get that thing going, you know, Upstairs or no Upstairs. It's all fixed up, just needs feeding with information. We could save ourselves a lot of writing up.' He rose and wandered over to the computer screen, his back to Claire, who longed to reach out and touch him. For luck, perhaps, for all the patients with a poor prognosis, those in pain, those with aching hearts. . .

'Claire?' Suddenly he was beside her, though she hadn't been aware of movement. Her eyes were filled with tears, and hastily she wiped them on her apron. 'Oh, Claire, my darling, don't cry! I can't bear it.' Strong arms enfolded her, and wearily she rested her head against his chest, the cap getting crumpled in the process.

'Sorry, I just felt down, that's all I —— ' Claire began, wanting to talk about Wendy, then the office phone went and John reached it first. His expression changed even as she watched, and he almost flung the receiver at her.

'For you, Staff Nurse — can you ensure that you don't take personal calls on the ward in future?' Then John was gone, a distraught Claire watching the door

swing to behind him. A voice crackled from the other
end of the telephone, and she said, 'Westfield Ward,
Staff Nurse speaking. Can I help you?' in rather a
dazed voice.

'I hope I didn't interrupt a ward-round, Nurse
Claire.' David Dunster's voice came across clearly,
and Claire wished him on the moon. 'No, it's too late
for that, isn't it?' he went on. 'Look, about next
Friday—could we make it Thursday instead? I'll have
to take work home that weekend, or so I've been told.'

'What? No, really, don't worry about taking me to
lunch,' Claire said, still in that dazed voice. John had
called her his darling! 'My reward is in seeing patients
go out cured, you know. There's no need to wine and
dine me as an extra reward! I hope your gran goes on
well,' she rushed on, effectively preventing him from
arguing. 'All the best, Mr Dunster. Cheerio.' She put
the receiver down, her eyes misting over. *Did* he
actually call her 'my darling'? When he had suggested
living together, was it because he loved her?

For a moment Claire had visions of becoming the
surgeon's wife, of making a home, a proper home, for
Katy and the boys. Then the vision faded as her
practical self came to the fore. Whatever John had in
mind, it wasn't marriage. Even if he was thinking
along those lines, Katy would find some way of spoiling
the relationship, that was for sure! And the boys—
what did she know about bringing up children? All in
all, it would be better for John's children if he and
Tania did get back together. Perhaps Katy had the
right idea.

She rose, remade her cap, gave a tug to her apron,
then marched out. Wendy must be visited, cheered up
if possible, then there was the ward work to finish—
her broken heart was of little consequence.

CHAPTER TEN

'THIS is going to be my computer-room. I've got the printer set up — oh, mind you don't trip,' John called out as Claire gingerly picked her way through the piles of books and stationery, then followed him into a big, sunny room overlooking the rear garden. This, then was to be his base for the short while he remained at the District. When summer ended, he would go, and Claire's gaze was anguished as it rested upon him.

He swung round, as if aware of her wayward thoughts, and Claire gave him her cheery smile. 'If it were me, I'd be tempted to waste time gazing out at the flowers. I wouldn't get any work done on my book,' she said hurriedly, as his level gaze held hers. 'It's a nice big garden for the children, though — you could put up a hidey-house for them. *I* always wanted a tree-house but Dad wouldn't let me have one!'

John chuckled. 'Bit of a tomboy, were you? You shock me, Staff Nurse! Make yourself at home while I find a kettle and somewhere to plug it in.' He waved a hand to indicate the cluttered room, then disappeared from view, but Claire followed him into the kitchen. This was small but had an alcove at the end with just enough room for a table and two chairs.

It was an older house, one of those situated at the opposite end of the village, about as far away from Hemsley Manor as one could get yet still be within the parish, though only a few minutes from her own home. She had been astonished when, the previous day, John had asked if she would like to see over his temporary home, and had visualised one of the Medhursts' cottages or even a trailer! Even with a family, the Red House was far too large and sprawling, particularly as John seemed to spend more time at the hospital than anywhere else. Surely Katy would be lonely?

'Will you have a housekeeper?' Claire asked curiously as she put out two brightly coloured mugs. 'Katy will be lonely, especially since her mum will be away. And what —— ?'

'What about the boys?' John finished the sentence for her. 'I wasn't going to mention them again, but —— '

Now it was Claire's turn to butt in on him. 'Not going to mention them! You don't seem to care! No, I'm sorry,' she said simply. 'Where's the milk? I can't see a fridge — oh, it's small, isn't it?' She peered down at the fridge she had belatedly discovered tucked away in a corner. 'What about a freezer?'

'Yes, I shall get a freezer, never fear, Staff Nurse.' Thankfully, John sounded exasperated rather than angry, as he had every right to be, Claire reflected, as they sat companionably at the table. She warmed her hands on the mug, trying desperately to think of something non-contentious to say. Finding nothing, she remained silent.

It was John who broke the silence. 'You wanted to talk about the boys, and we will. I think this has gone on long enough —— ' he began, but Claire chipped in,

'No, I don't want to talk about your family, not really, but you seem to think people are material for experiments, even Katy! You've taken over the role of both parents, but she's allowed to run wild, as far as I can see. She needs company, John!'

'I do not experiment on people!' John was obviously keeping his feelings well under control. 'Katy's under the watchful eye of Mrs Taylor and she doesn't run wild, but a twelve-year-old girl isn't a child these days. She knows she has to mind what I say, and she'll be going to a new school in September. And I interview patients,' he went on remorselessly, 'because I genuinely want to *know* what they're feeling about the nursing or medical care they've received. I can't write a textbook which will help the nurses or junior doctors of the future unless I talk to patients.'

'Mrs Smith was worried because you asked her such a lot of questions,' Claire said stubbornly, 'and she's got enough problems as it is! Mr Smith's going on —— '

'"As well as can be expected",' John put in. 'What exactly does that phrase summon up in your mind? No, don't tell me as a nurse, tell me how it strikes you as a relative.'

Claire thought for a moment. 'To me, it means that after investigations or operation the patient is as we would expect him to be, but I can see that it doesn't really mean anything to a lay person. *How* well is "as well as can be expected"?'

He nodded, putting his mug down with a thump and rising, his gaze enigmatic. 'Exactly, but I've heard at least three nurses use that expression, and it won't do, Claire. We have to think of the relatives as well as the patients, just as you suggested. Too often they're ignored. That's something that will go in my book. I'm halfway through it, by the way.' He yawned, and Claire got up, belatedly remembering that he had spent most of the day in Theatre and must be wanting to rest. And she'd accused him of not caring about his patients!

'I'd better go—Suzanne might come home this evening. She could be there already.' Yes, that was a point. It wouldn't do if her cousin found out she'd been in the surgeon's new home.

'Come on a quick Cook's tour of the rest of the house, then,' John suggested, and Claire followed him through to a small, sparsely furnished dining-room. The woodwork was dark, oak-stained, and the room needed a woman's touch, Claire considered, but perhaps Stella Pountney. . .?

'There's an old-fashioned bathroom plus four bedrooms. It's too big for us,' John went on, echoing her earlier thoughts, 'but it has potential, as the letting agent assured me! I think he was hoping to sell it after my tenancy is up.'

'It wouldn't be worth you buying it if you're off back to London afterwards,' Claire said slowly, then winced, recalling John's offer. 'Oh, is this Katy's room?'

They were upstairs by then, and the late summer sun was casting shadows already. Summer was more than half over, Claire reminded herself. August, the dying of the year. . .

'That's right, this is Katy's room — tidier than it will be when she moves in!' John said ruefully. 'I'm at the other end of the house, as far away from her ghetto-blaster as possible! She can have another of the bedrooms as a study. . .' He paused, his eyes on Claire, who turned, puzzled.

'Won't the boys want a room each? It's always what Katy wants! She's rather like the character in Susan Coolidge's "What Katy Did" books I used to read as a child.'

'Oh? And what *did* Katy do in the books?' John ran a hand through his hair in a weary gesture. 'Don't tell me she was as harum-scarum as my daughter?'

'Yes, she was. Always up to scrapes until she had an accident, then she ran the household from her bed! There was *What Katy Did*, *What Katy Did at School*, and. . . Oh, yes, *What Katy Did Next*. They were classics, real American homespun stories, and I loved them,' Claire went on.

'What did Katy do next? That sounds intriguing! Didn't drive her father grey with worry, did she?'

'Oh, no, she was grown-up by then — she got married.'

'My Katy's too young to inflict that kind of punishment upon some poor guy,' John said with feeling. 'I don't intend to get trapped into marriage again. Let's go downstairs, if you've seen everything? Or would you like me to show you *my* room?'

Still reeling from his remark about marriage, Claire ignored the last part. Now she'd had it spelled out for her, hadn't she? Marriage was definitely out. 'No, I'd better go. You've had a hard day, then there was Wendy. . .' Her voice trailed away.

'We caught her at an earlier stage than Mr Upshall. I think most of her poor appetite *was* due to depression,' John said gently. 'As you know, nil appetite is a late sign in gastric carcinoma, but some of her problems were digestive. She eats with her mouth open, had you noticed? Swallowing air all the while —

then she's got this morbid fear of constipation, and keeps dosing herself up. She thinks she's constipated if twenty-four hours go by without a motion! Then out come the purgatives. It's no wonder she's always in discomfort. I know how much you care for that lady, and that's why I invited you along this evening. At least it's taken your mind off operations.' As he spoke, John was halfway down the stairs, and Claire followed slowly. He was right, as he usually was. And it proved he cared enough for her to try to divert her attention. That was *some* small comfort.

'It must be boring to be right so often, but yes, I *did* need human company,' she acknowledged. 'Can I wash up the mugs? Yes, I will,' she went on, making her way to the kitchen. John followed her, leaning against the door-jamb, his thoughts apparently sombre ones, for, when Claire met his gaze, those intensely blue eyes were sad.

'Claire,' he began, then paused, while she waited, tea-towel clutched in one hand. '*Are* you spending Sunday with Martin?'

'No — he's going back to Suffolk to see his wife. He rang her and she cried down the phone! He's over the moon because she missed him. He was going to write,' Claire went on, remembering Martin's request for assistance, 'but I'm glad he phoned her.'

John smiled, a smile of such genuine warmth that Claire thought the sun was shining into the dark kitchen. 'I'm glad — I didn't want you to throw yourself away on a married man.'

'Or a divorced one?' she suggested, wondering how she could sound so calm when her heart was racing away painfully.

'Or a divorced one,' he agreed, his smile fading. 'You're too good for us both, Claire, and I shouldn't have asked you to go away with me,' he said stiffly, while Claire just stared. 'You deserve better than me — how about that guy who used to visit his granny? He seems keen.'

'According to his gran, *he's* married as well. All the best ones marry young,' Claire said lightly, trying not to show her anguish. 'The world is full of married men looking for someone like me!'

'There isn't anyone like you, Claire—you're unique.' John paused, then shrugged, a helpless, almost defeated gesture that tore at Claire's heartstrings.

'Don't—please!' she begged, and, before she could think better of it, she ran towards him, arms outstretched. He gazed at her for a long, long moment, then held out his own arms and Claire snuggled against him, her face raised for his kiss.

But he didn't kiss her. Instead, his lips found an erogenous place just behind her ear, and she sighed blissfully. Oh, she knew this would be just a brief interlude for him. He didn't love her, had no serious intentions, but at least he wasn't like Martin, letting her believe that he cared, that one day they would marry, have a proper home, a place where they could settle down, have a little Katy, Robert and Johnnie. . . John was offering her nothing at all, but she was offering him her love, her whole heart, body and soul, for she could do no less. She threw her heart into everything she did, into her care of the patients, even the nourishing of the ever increasing numbers of plants she tended. Such was her way, and she hoped John understood that. Perhaps, too, she might go to London with him. Surely she could try to befriend Katy?

'Claire, do you know what I need more than anything else? Right at this moment?' John murmured, his lips slowly and sensuously working their way up to the corner of her mouth, which he kissed gently.

Unable to speak, Claire shook her head, then heard his sigh. 'A good sleep! I've been on my feet most of the day, and I've had to tell two patients that what I've done is merely palliative, that I can't cure them. Then you fall into my arms, hoping for a romantic interlude! I can't, Claire; I'm sorry, but I haven't the energy left to raise a leg, let alone anything else!'

Claire chuckled. 'Then you shall have a good sleep! And I'll watch over you.' Her own needs could wait.

John was her patient for the time being and would have to obey her!

For a moment they clung together, then, hand in hand, they walked slowly up the winding staircase, pausing every now and then to kiss. John's bedroom contained a narrow bed covered with a duvet, the only other furniture being a double wardrobe and a couple of chairs, and Claire raised a brow. 'A bit spartan, isn't it?' As she spoke, she patted the bed invitingly, and, with a grin, John took off his trainers then stretched out on the bed while she tenderly laid the duvet on top of him. 'Pillows?'

'Hmm? Oh, just one, thank you, Nurse. They're in the airing cupboard,' he murmured drowsily, his eyes already closing.

John hadn't thought to tell her where the airing cupboard was to be found, but she finally located it in the hall by the sitting-room. She glanced about her before going back upstairs. If the furniture had come with the house, she didn't think much of it. It was all old and grim-looking. There was little of it as well, certainly not enough to make a comfortable home for three children.

Frowning a bit at thought of the children and wondering uneasily where a certain Katy was, Claire took two pillows and a blanket and sheet up to the bedroom, to find her romantic hero dead to the world.

In sleep John's hard features were relaxed, and he looked young and innocent as he lay there. Only a tell-tale streak of grey in his dark hair marked the passage of the years, and Claire put out a hand to stroke his hair then stopped, fearful of waking him. He needed sleep after his eventful day, and it was selfish of her not to have realised that. Her own busy shift had left her feeling weary, but it was nothing compared with his day. She gazed at the bed and the sleeping man for an instant, then tiptoed away to Katy's room where she snuggled down under a duvet patterned with hairy young men carrying guitars!

It was dusk when she awoke, and she sat up suddenly, wondering uneasily for a moment where she was. Was she due on duty? And whose bed was this? Groaning a little, she eased the duvet off, then almost jumped out of her skin when a soft chuckle reached her from the doorway. 'Enjoy your sleep, Staff Nurse? You'll be late on duty,' John said, laughter in his voice.

Claire thought for a moment. 'No, you can't catch me like that! I've *been* on duty—I've got all the aches and pains to prove it, and my feet hurt. I'd better go— you don't want Katy coming in search of you and finding someone in her bed, like the Three Bears!' She felt around for her sandals, then they were taken from her, and John cupped her bare foot in his warm hands. The warmth shot right up her leg and through her body, and she tensed, wanting him so much. Wanting and needing to comfort him as well as herself. Yet he was weary and she mustn't be selfish.

'Let go of my foot, please, sir—Sister Pountney might come in at any moment,' she said with a smile in her voice.

'Good lord, I hope not!' John said with feeling, but he didn't release her foot. Instead, he began to stroke it, his sensitive fingers causing the warmth to invade her whole body, and she could feel moistness between her thighs. He had no right to torment her like this!

'Don't, please, John,' she whispered, and abruptly he got up.

'I'm sorry—put it down to the summer evening and the close proximity of a bed,' he said flatly. 'I'll see you downstairs—I have a feeling we've both been missed by now.'

Oh, no, he wasn't going like that! Still in her bare feet, Claire padded out after him, clutching at his shirt as he reached the landing. 'You've no right to torment me! You don't want me but I——' No, she couldn't say that. It made her sound like some kind of groupie, always panting after sex. To her, it was *love*, and she wanted so much to give that love to John, to have the release that their act of union would bring. He hadn't the right to deny her that!

'Are you sure, Claire?' he asked tenderly, as somehow she found herself in his arms. Taking her contented sigh for assent, he swept her up and cradled her to his chest for a moment, his smile slow, sensual, stirring her innermost being, then he carried her to his own bedroom, pausing to kiss her as they crossed the threshold.

How wonderful it would be if she were a bride, all in white lace with a long flowing veil, and this really were the threshold of their home, Claire thought dreamily, then all conscious thought was swept away as he lowered her on to that uncomfortable-looking bed which was still warm from his sleep.

John looked down at her with those intense blue eyes. 'Oh, Claire!' Her name was said almost in despair, and she reached up and brushed her lips against his, only to be caught and held fiercely against his chest. She could feel his heart thudding against her own, feel his laughter, too.

'There isn't a lot of room for manoeuvre, Staff Nurse,' he murmured against her ear. 'I apologise for the unromantic surroundings!'

'We ought to have a four-poster bed with those lace-edged pillows and satin sheets you were on about,' Claire agreed, 'but this is much cosier — don't you think so, sir?'

'You could be right, Staff Nurse. I'll have to ask Upstairs what they think!' They giggled together like a couple of children, then there was no more laughter as their lips met gently, tentatively at first. Claire pressed closer to him as his lips moved away from hers and explored her cheek, her neck, her throat. He pushed aside the bright, glossy hair to explore the skin behind her earlobe. 'You have delicious ears — do you know that?'

Claire murmured her agreement, trying to retain some measure of detachment from the sensations threatening to swamp her, but her hunger for closeness and warmth were turning into physical desire too powerful to deny. Yet she was aware of the sensation of being *loved*, of being in the arms of a man who loved, who cherished her. But that wasn't so — hadn't

he made that plain enough? Sex, the physical release
that their union would bring, that was all a certain
consultant surgeon desired. Her love would have to be
enough for both of them; she would simply have to
pretend that she believed him to love her.

John's sensitive fingers began a slow and tender
exploration of the contours of her body through the
thin T-shirt, sending ripple after ripple of melting
sensation coursing through her whole being. Then,
impatient of the clothes that kept them apart, they
helped each other undress, the heat shooting through
Claire's body as John kissed her breasts once her T-
shirt and flimsy bra were flung to one side. Then,
slowly and almost reverently, he eased her jeans down,
Claire kicking her panties off, before reaching for his
shirt buttons.

Then bare flesh moved against bare flesh, and Claire
drew in a quivering breath, her mouth suddenly dry
with desire. Hardly knowing what she was doing, she
drew his dark head down to her breasts, a gasp
breaking from her as John's tongue encircled her
nipple. His arms tightened about her and she caught
her breath as the warmth of his body filled her with a
spasm of pure pleasure. They kissed, Claire releasing
all the hunger and longing pent up inside her. She felt
his own hunger, was overpowered by it, then he joined
his body wholly to hers and carried her into another
world, a world so utterly, wonderfully different that
her senses spun and she could feel herself whirling
through space. . .

Afterwards, as she was held close in John's arms,
she felt such a sense of peace and contentment that
she wanted to weep tears of pure joy. He nuzzled her
hair, seemingly reluctant to let her go, not turning
away and groping for cigarettes, as Martin had once
done—until she had told him he must either give up
smoking or give up her! He had, Claire reflected
without bitterness, given up both.

'Penny for your thoughts, Staff Nurse,' John said
teasingly, his warm breath on her face.

'I was just thinking of Martin,' Claire said unwisely,

then paused, horrified at what he must think she meant. 'Oh, no! What I mean is——'

'Comparing our performances, were you?' Now ice had replaced the warmth, and John swung his legs out of the bed, leaving Claire cold and bereft. 'How do I rate? Before you award me points, bear in mind that I've had a busy day and might not be up to my usual standard!'

'John, no!' But he had snatched up his clothes and was out of the door before Claire could reach him. Then, aware of her own nakedness, she glanced about for her own clothes. She felt at a disadvantage like this. Then her eyes widened in dismay. Voices!

She crept to the door and peered over the banister. Whoever it was must have come round by the back door. Men's voices, thankfully. At least Katy hadn't caught her father in his birthday suit! A hysterical giggle broke from her, hastily stifled. The sooner she got dressed the better. Perhaps it was someone from the hospital. . .

Thrusting her feet into her sandals, Claire hastily smoothed down the bed once she was dressed, and crept out to the landing. Dared she risk it? Only John's car was out front since he'd given her a lift. She could easily walk home, but would John get rid of whoever it was? If he was pretending to be alone and she calmly walked downstairs, it would cause embarrassment all round.

Then there was a hammering at the front-door knocker, deciding the matter for her. Now there was no escape! The wages of sin indeed. If she hadn't practically forced John to make love to her, none of this would have happened. She would have been at home now, chattering to Suzanne, innocently eating her supper and. . . And I would have missed the greatest experience of my life, Claire mused, as she waited to see who would answer the door. John might have been weary, but it was in no way reflected in his performance. He needn't worry about comparisons with Martin Medhurst!

Then footsteps, and Claire leaned further over.

John, calling over his shoulder to——Martin! 'I'll go, Martin. It's probably someone from the hospital,' he called loudly, but Claire couldn't hear what Martin replied. Then John glanced up the stairs, meeting Claire's anguished gaze. He gestured, which Claire interpreted to mean that she should escape out of the front door once he'd brought whoever it was into the house. Then the knocker went again, and someone began banging on the door as John opened it.

Claire dodged back into the shadows. Katy! And would the sharp-eyed 'What Katy Did' know what *they* had done? Claire rather thought she would.

'Hello, poppet. Not thinking of bringing up a batter-ing-ram, were you?' John's voice was stern. 'I got to the door as fast as I could.'

'Sorry, Daddy. I thought something had happened to you.' There was suspicion in Katy's voice, and Claire hardly dared breathe. She couldn't be seen, but all the girl needed to do was dart upstairs to see her room, then. . . Thankfully, she didn't and their voices faded as they went into the back of the house.

Claire let out her pent-up breath. Now for the difficult part. Carefully avoiding the centre of the stairs, which she had noted creaked a little, she took off her sandals then inched her way down, hoping she hadn't left anything incriminating in the bedroom. Luck was on her side and she eased her way out of the door and was running down the front path and out through the double gates as if Satan himself were after her.

Hot and bothered and very, very tired, Claire walked slowly home, hoping that this was one Friday Suzanne would decide to stay in London. It wasn't, and Claire groaned as she came upon the well-lit house. Now there would be an inquest.

'Claire, what *have* you been up to? Or shouldn't I ask?' Suzanne's expression was shrewd, and Claire coloured. 'Had to run for it, did you?' her cousin went on, and chuckled. After a moment, Claire joined in and they sank on to the settee and laughed themselves into a coughing fit.

'Oh, Suzanne! It's not funny really, but. . .' Claire gurgled, then made a supreme effort to sober up. It wasn't as if she'd had anything to drink! 'Laughter is the best medicine, Staff Nurse Shaw says,' she said crisply, getting up. 'I need a shower and an early night. It's been one of those days. Oh ——' She turned back to Suzanne, who was eyeing her complacently. 'You didn't say you were definitely coming home for the weekend! Has anything interesting happened?'

'Well. . .' Suzanne hesitated, then slipped a hand down her neckline, producing a sparkling diamond solitaire on a gold chain, which she held out. 'There! I've decided that marriage *has* got a lot to offer after all! Reggie and I are going to get married, at Christmas, we thought, then he's off to New York and I'm going with him.'

She must have misinterpreted Claire's stricken expression, because she jumped up and rushed over. 'Claire, I'm sorry! I had no right to spring this on you, but I've been dying to tell you all the way home! You can come over on holiday, and it's not a permanent placement! We'll be back to live in London. You haven't lost me altogether,' Suzanne babbled on, and Claire found herself soothing her cousin, as so often in the past.

Never mind Nurse Shaw's problems, there was always someone worse off. Tell your troubles to Nurse Shaw, tell her that marriage has a lot to offer — she might even agree with you.

At length, Claire managed to escape and plodded ever so slowly upstairs to the sanctuary of her bedroom. Yes, marriage *did* have a lot to offer, but unfortunately no one wanted to marry her.

CHAPTER ELEVEN

GOING on duty on Saturday morning was something of an anticlimax after the events of Friday, and for once Claire was reluctant to set foot on the ward. There was no telling what time John would stroll on to Westfield. What could she say to the man? Her cheeks felt heated just at the thought of meeting him.

Still, duty called. Not a lot happened at weekends on Surgical, and they weren't on 'take', but that didn't mean they wouldn't see John Colby.

'Isn't John a dream? It makes me wish I were on days,' Maria, the relief night nurse commented as she filled Claire in on the events of the night. In contrast to Bibi, Maria evidently found John an improvement on the dour registrar!

Claire's smile was non-committal. 'Sometimes he is. I think it depends on how he gets on in Theatre.' Then she frowned. 'He wasn't here last night, surely?' she went on, as memory of what the surgeon had been doing last night came flooding back. 'He went off duty at five.'

'Oh, yes, he came back.' Maria beamed, her dark eyes flashing. 'Perhaps it was to see me! He saw all his patients, though, but he said he'd come back to take a look at a patient in Camber, really. Said she was special, but I don't know who that was.'

'Wendy Clark,' Claire said wonderingly. John had looked in on Wendy because she was special to a certain staff nurse! Now it was her turn to beam, and Maria eyed her speculatively.

'Friendly with him, are we? Now let's have a quick rundown then I'd like to get away on time. Steve Smith —' Maria tapped her nail against his name on the Kardex '— slept badly, fretting about this and that. Or the other,' she said meaningly. 'Seems he and his wife haven't had sex for some months. He told the

162

male nurse that, not me. It's obviously bugging him, and he's still an "ulcer personality", anyway. Refused sedation and asked to see Nurse Claire. Told she would be on first thing in the morning,' Maria went on, reading from her notes. 'Oh, by the way, this is for you, from that spotty young man we took in for Rye Ward. He called in just after you'd gone. Says to tell you he's passed his stone and been discharged.' Maria handed over a big tin of chocolate biscuits. 'You get all the presents,' she complained, and Claire smirked.

'You're just jealous because you love chocolate biscuits. We'll share them between the three shifts, so don't worry,' Claire said with a smile. 'I'm glad he's all right now. I liked him, really.'

'You like them all, old and young. Old Mr Peel's back, by the way. Oh, you didn't know him, did you? He's lovely; we had him a few months back for obs but couldn't find anything except his bowels. These old ones don't eat their greens or their bran! He's an acute abdomen—suspected appendix with possible peritonitis was the diagnosis. Gram took him down to Theatre and he was right. Gram's becoming more human under the guidance of the dishy Colby, I think.' Maria raised her eyes questioningly, and Claire hoped her blush didn't show. If anyone in the hospital got an inkling that the innocent-looking Staff Nurse Shaw had lain naked in the arms of the 'dishy Colby', she would run away! The flush deepened, and Maria's eyes narrowed but she didn't comment, to Claire's relief.

'Rotherfield's on "take" but Gram offered a bed to Mr Peel, so I hope that will be OK,' the night nurse finished, before throwing the keys on the desk and giving Claire a big smile. 'Be good, Staff Nurse Claire! I hear all the gossip, don't forget!'

Once she had allocated duties for the morning, Claire slipped over to Camber to assess Wendy's progress after her gastrectomy. Wendy still looked dehydrated yet seemed more cheerful than of late. It was the relief of knowing that she had a physical illness, of being aware that all the inconclusive investigations, the dismissal of her as a 'chronic depression with constipation', were at an end. Claire knew Wendy didn't realise the seriousness of her condition, and had agreed with John that she might not be able to cope with the knowledge. Gastric carcinoma had a poor prognosis, sometimes only weeks of life being left after the symptoms had first presented, but where there was life there was hope. Claire could hear John's words in her head, as she stroked Wendy's hand.

'I hear Mr Colby's pleased with you,' she said.

'Yes, he came to see me last night — lateish, it was. Said he'd had a busy evening but, knowing as I was special, he'd come to give me a look-in. . .' Wendy's tired voice trailed off, and Claire left her to sleep. Mr Colby had certainly had a busy evening, and she only hoped Wendy never found out how busy!

Remembering that Steve Smith wanted to see her, Claire made him her second stop on her round, Mr Peel being still asleep. Mrs Smith had bravely shrugged off her personal problems and taken Claire's advice to heart about not expecting her husband to die any second, and Claire felt the woman's visits helped now. But how difficult it must be to live with an 'ulcer personality', a constant worrier, a person who fired up over the least thing. Add that to their financial and sexual worries, and Claire thought Mrs Smith deserved a medal for coping as well as she had.

'How did you sleep, Mr Smith?' Claire smiled down at the man in question, who sighed gustily.

'I was just about to shave, but I knew you would come eventually.' Mr Smith laid emphasis on the last word, but Claire ignored that. He must know how busy mornings were on a surgical ward. He wasn't, in any case, in a hurry to go places. 'I didn't sleep too well, but who would, propped up?' he went on, his dark grey, almost black eyes fixed intently upon Claire.

'That's to prevent fluid in the —' Claire began, but he waved her to silence.

'You've explained all that before. Or someone has. They keep telling me things, then they go into a huddle with Jenny and God only know what they tell *her*!'

'Much the same as we tell you, I imagine,' Claire

said calmly. 'You nearly died, Mr Smith. You might at
least be grateful that the surgeon saved you and that
our nursing is keeping you alive. You'll be fine in a
little while,' she went on, seeing his look of amazement
that anyone should speak to him like that, 'but if you
haven't anything specific to ask me I *do* have a ward
to run. Shall I ask Sister to see you when she comes
on duty?' Claire smiled her innocent, cheerful smile,
and Mr Smith shrugged.

'That smile will get you anything, and I expect it
does,' he said unexpectedly.

'Not always,' Claire said, her smile rueful this time.
If only it did! 'I hope you're getting up after breakfast?
Mr Colby says you can begin a light diet today, then a
full gastric diet in a day or so,' she went on.

'I suppose that means I'll be discharged once I can
tolerate meals?' he said miserably.

'We do need the bed, Mr Smith, but don't worry,
we won't send you out a minute before we have to,'
Claire assured him, before going on to the rest of the
cubicle. Another patient who didn't want to leave the
sanctuary of hospital! He no longer needed the intra-
venous infusion or the naso-gastric tube so he should
be well on the mend. He——

Thoughts of Mr Smith's ulcer went out of her head
when she saw a tall, athletic figure she knew rather
well. As always, sight of him sent her BP over the top,
and she hardly knew what to say. How difficult it was
to come down to earth, to be nurse and surgeon again,
when only hours before they had been locked in a
passionate embrace!

John made it easier, his gaze sombre as it rested
upon her. Gone was the passionate, demanding man
of Friday night. 'I've come in to see Alan Keates, Staff
Nurse—is that convenient?' His voice was cool, the
voice of a stranger, and Claire's heart broke anew.

'Yes, of course, he's in the dayroom. I——' She
broke off, then laid a small hand on his arm. 'I hope
everything went well last night?' she hurried on.
'About Katy, I mean. She didn't. . .' She left the

sentence unfinished, hastily snatching her hand away as voices approached, then passed.

'Didn't suspect her aged father might have a sex life? No, I don't think so,' he said thoughtfully. 'Parents are past that sort of thing!' His stern features relaxed in a faint smile. 'She and Martin got worried about me when darkness fell and I failed to return. She convinced him that I'd fallen through a rotten floorboard, so he had to give her a lift down just to make sure I hadn't. Knowing Katy, I should be grateful she didn't summon the police and an ambulance!'

'It's good to know she worries about her aged father. Most teenagers wouldn't bother,' Claire said quietly, then went on, 'What about Katy, anyway?'

'Yes, what about Katy?' John sighed, then flopped down into a chair at the nurses' station, his eyes fixed intently on Claire's face. 'Now that Justin's dead, Katy told me it's time I started thinking about remarriage. With Tania, naturally.'

'Justin—is that who Miss Wallace is grieving for? She was going to marry him?' Claire guessed.

'Yes, they were very much in love, though I don't think my daughter understood that. Justin died during open-heart surgery and that broke Tania up. She was all for coming here straight away, though, but I persuaded her to take time to mourn properly. Justin had two sons and she's getting to know them now, while I supposedly take care of Katy—they're the brothers she always wanted and we denied her.'

'They're Robert and Johnnie?' Everything began to fit into place. Poor, lonely Katy, who had to invent brothers!

John smiled quizzically. 'No, Justin junior and Andrew. Ah, you've been talking to Katy!'

'She told me about Robert and Johnnie, her brothers aged eight and ten. But you said you have two boys!' It wasn't just Katy—John himself had misled her.

'When Katy sees me with a personable young woman, she immediately senses danger. She started that "Mummy and the boys will be waiting" nonsense, and I suppose I played along with her. It's saved me from a few man-eaters in my time!' he admitted.

'Including Suzanne, yes. I can see that, but why didn't you tell me?'

'I tried to, several times, if I remember rightly,' he said, then he rose and gazed down at her. 'Then I thought it was probably better if you didn't know about the mythical boys. After all, there was no point in you taking me seriously, so —'

'I've no intention of taking you seriously! I understand about last night,' Claire said sharply, determined not to break down in so public a place. 'It was fun for me too, you know — I awarded you ten out of ten! And for you it was a little light relief after the trauma of Theatre, I imagine.'

'No, Claire! Don't say that. It wasn't —' But Claire, straight-backed and determined, walked quickly away. She didn't want to hear any excuses. She had been an interlude in his busy life, nothing more.

John did his round, as usual, but they were nurse and consultant again so that made it easier to cope with, and once Sister Pountney made her appearance Claire had no need even to enter the office, let alone liaise with the consultant. She told herself she was glad. Of course she was glad! He had no right to tell her there was no point in taking him seriously. Hadn't he already made that plain enough?

Swallowing the lump in her throat, Claire prepared to go off duty. But before she changed she must visit Wendy again, who, as usual now, had Sam by her side.

'That nice Mr Colby's coming back to see me — he promised,' Wendy said, clutching Sam's hand. 'Me and Sam, we're going to get married, dear, though me family don't know it yet,' she confided. 'He needs somebody to take care of him, don't you, Sam?'

Sam, a grizzly-haired man of about seventy, nodded. 'I reckon I do.'

'I'm delighted for you! Sam will give you an interest in life,' Claire said warmly. 'Mr Colby's left the ward, though. There's an emergency somewhere, so don't be disappointed if he can't get back to you,' Claire warned.

'He promised,' Wendy said stubbornly, 'and he'll never let anyone down, not if he promised. You could do worse than get wed to him, young Claire.' Wendy closed her eyes and Claire moved away. Yes, she could so a lot worse than wed the surgeon, but who wanted a reluctant bridegroom? And, moreover, a bridegroom who couldn't even take the trouble to ring to make sure she had got home safely! That hurt, more than Claire was prepared to admit.

Suzanne was staying just for Saturday, returning to London early on Sunday to be with Reggie, so they dined out that night in Elmleigh. Claire merely picked at her food, though, and Suzanne berated her for not cheering up.

'I know you'll miss me, my pet, but you've never travelled much and you'll love New York! We might even get you fixed up with a nice American,' Suzanne said, her smile glowing.

'Yes, that would be lovely.' Claire smiled and sipped her coffee, listening with only half an ear. She would be lonely without Suzanne. The house would have to go, for a start. Yes, it was time for new beginnings, and she would make one herself.

With that thought in mind, she rose immediately after Suzanne had finished. 'I've had an awful day — you won't mind if we go home now, Suzanne? I——' What else she was about to say went out of her head, for now she had a good view of the restaurant she saw a family group in one corner that she recognised. Suzanne's eyes followed hers.

'Aha! I spy your consultant surgeon and daughter — *and* with a woman! She's pretty — is that his wife?' Suzanne craned her neck for a better view.

'Er. . .' Claire could hardly pretend not to know. 'Oh, no, he isn't married now. She's his ex-wife, my new surgeon, Miss Wallace. She'll come to the District when he leaves,' Clare admitted reluctantly, and Suzanne's eyes swivelled back to hers. In them was dawning comprehension.

'I should have known! Oh, Claire, I'm so sorry! I rather fancied him when we met in the park, you know, but it was obvious he didn't even see me!' Suzanne sounded so aggrieved that Claire wanted to laugh. Hadn't she thought the very same thing about Suzanne—that John wouldn't see *her* if she was with Suzanne?

'You were with *him* last night, weren't you?' Suzanne said as they made their way out of the restaurant into the still, warm night. John had seen them, and Claire had been conscious of his eyes following her as she left. What would Katy and her mother make of that? she wondered.

'Yes, we were together last night, and Katy nearly caught us, so it serves me right, I suppose,' Claire said with a rueful smile as they walked over to the car. 'He never even phoned to see if I'd arrived home safely!' she went on, without meaning to. It sounded childish, really. After all, nothing much could happen to her in Hemsley Green.

'He did phone,' her cousin said, as she eased herself behind the wheel, and Claire just stared at her. 'You'd gone up to bed and I wasn't going to disturb you. And. . .' She shrugged. 'He was obviously ringing from the hospital, so I said yes, you were home, that you'd had a riotous evening and we'd. . .'

'Yes?' Claire prompted, dread settling on her. 'What exactly *did* you say?'

'I told him we'd had a damn good laugh! Oh, Claire, I'm sorry, but I thought he was taking advantage of you and I wanted to teach him a lesson! I did it for you, pet,' Suzanne went on anxiously, and Claire could have shaken her.

Instead, she drew a long shuddering breath. 'I see,' was all she could find to say. There was no point in quarrelling with Suzanne. It would only spoil her cousin's happiness and put a damper on their relationship. More importantly, what was said couldn't be unsaid. Let John think what he liked! It really didn't matter.

* * *

'Mrs Plumpton's coming back for her op.' John glanced up from the case-notes he was perusing, catching Claire unawares, and she took a moment to bring her thoughts back.

'Oh, to Camber? I'm glad,' she said warmly, 'but what about Mr Plumpton?'

The look John gave her was cool. 'She didn't mention him, but she seemed in a happier frame of mind, so I arranged with the GP to have her back for her cholecystectomy. She asked if you would be there, so I told her you'd moved next door but would pop in to see her,' John went on, and Claire nodded.

'Of course I will. I liked her — one of those tough Tynesiders my father used to admire! He did part of his training in Northumbria and had a great admiration for the people.' Yes, that was an idea. Since last Friday, she had given a lot of thought to her future. She would move directly John went, and why not the North? Now that Suzanne was crossing an ocean to live, nothing really kept her in Sussex except memories. And they would fade, eventually.

'Claire!' John said sharply, and Claire looked her surprise. 'Your face then, it went. . .' He hesitated. 'I don't know. The memory was an unhappy one and you're too young to have unhappy memories.'

'Unhappiness isn't the prerogative of the elderly,' she retorted. 'Life isn't simple for any of us. We all have painful recollections,' she went on, after a moment, and John put out a hand as if to comfort her, then dropped it again. They were alone in the Westfield office, but they could be disturbed at any moment.

'Now isn't the time for baring the soul, but come to a pot-luck supper at the Red House. I've almost finished moving in now — you can try out the word processor,' John suggested.

Supper alone with John — or with John and Katy? Claire wondered. 'I don't finish until nine-thirty, and I'll be dead-beat by then, so I'd rather not, if you don't mind,' she said politely, glad that it was the truth and not some lie she'd had to think up on the spur of the moment.

'Yes, I do mind! There's something I want to say to you — but don't worry, your virtue will be quite safe.' Was that sarcasm in his voice? Claire didn't think so, and yet, by her own admission, she was far from innocent and had told him she rated his sexual performance highly. The man probably though she'd had umpteen lovers! Didn't he know what he was asking? How *could* she join him at his home and pretend nothing had happened? That electric charge that always seemed to be between them wouldn't go away merely because John wished it to.

'I can't! You don't know what you're asking!' she hissed, then rushed from the office, almost cannoning into Sister Pountney, who gave her a sharp look. That was all she needed!

When she saw Wendy that evening, she was met with, 'I hear you're a-going to have supper with that nice surgeon, dear!'

Claire blanched. 'Am I?' she said cautiously. 'I don't know where you got that idea, Wendy. I'm just off home! I'm on an early tomorrow, so I'll be here at seven.' Surely John hadn't told Wendy?

'Don't you go getting on your high horse with me, young Claire. I've known you since you was a baby. I told Mr Colby he ought to marry you and he's a-going to propose tonight!' She lay back, the picture of triumphant goodwill, but for a moment Claire could only stare.

'What have you been up to, Wendy?' With knees that felt suddenly weak, Claire sat by the bed and took Wendy's hands in hers. 'You haven't been naughty, have you?' she chided gently.

'Me? No! I jest told him he had a face as long as a fiddle and he needed that cheery Nurse Claire to put him right. You'd be better than a dose of salts for him,' Wendy went on, clearly regarding that as a great compliment, and Claire forced herself to smile. 'I says to him, Take your happiness while you can, Doctor —

I am. I've wasted too much time being poorly and such, worrying about me family, what this daughter would say, whether that daughter would go huffy, what my son might think. I had a rotten marriage before, but it's my life and I'm going to enjoy what's left to me.'

That brought tears to Claire's eyes, but in the dim lighting she hoped they would go unremarked. 'You didn't badger him to propose, did you, Wendy? He'll be terribly embarrassed.' Surely he *wasn't* going to propose marriage? Why he didn't even care for her! And what about Katy? Yes, indeed. With that sobering thought, Claire dropped a kiss on Wendy's brow and walked slowly and disconsolately out — to be hailed by a figure standing in the shadows between the two wards.

John came slowly towards her, and Claire hesitated. How could she face him now? And what *was* it he wanted to tell her? Attack was the best form of defence, or so she'd heard. 'Good evening, Mr Colby. I've just been to see Wendy — she seems to have been doing a bit of illicit match-making! I hope you didn't take her seriously?' With an effort, Claire kept a smile pinned to her face. Just as long as he didn't realise how much she cared! She would salvage her pride if nothing else. It was all he had left her.

He fell into step beside her. Since she could hardly outpace him, Claire had to accept his company. 'It seemed a good idea, Staff Nurse. Is it acceptable to you?' he said conversationally, and Claire gasped, but forced herself to keep walking since John didn't pause in his stride. It was almost as if he was discussing a business merger!

'No, it is not acceptable!' she cried. 'How could you think I'd marry you now?'

'You gave me top rating in the boudoir section, I seem to remember. If I fall short of perfection in other ways, no doubt you'll make allowances.' He stopped as they reached the head of the stairs, and paused, one hand on the rail. 'Will you, Claire?'

Claire was taken aback, her usual poise deserting

her, yet again, in John's presence. He was wearing a
dark suit and was freshly shaved, but he might have
been bare-chested and unshaven and decidedly unsettling, the way he had been on that first, memorable
meeting. His eyes were smiling at her, and for a
moment she could almost believe he meant it.

'Will I make allowances? I dare say I might,' she
hedged, 'but I have no intention of marrying. Nor
have you, I seem to remember,' she added, thrusting
out her chin in a determined way, as if hoping to head
him off. 'Wasn't it you who told me marriage was
overrated and——?'

'Yes, yes, I may have done,' he said testily, taking
her hand, which Claire tried unavailingly to free, 'and
I still hold that view,' he admitted, and this time Claire
did wrench free, making her way down the steep stairs
as quickly as she could. How dared he?

He who dared followed her, his long legs easily
overtaking hers, and he was at the bottom waiting for
her when she got to the ground floor. For a moment
she was tempted to run up the stairs again, but that
would be childish. 'You bring out the worst in me!'
She spoke her thoughts aloud, and the expression of
injured innocence on his face would have been almost
comical, if Claire had been in a laughing mood.

'You bring out the worst in me, too, but I won't
hold it against you,' he said, clearly amused.

'Good of you! If you'll excuse me, I've had a busy
day.' Claire made her way to the side-entrance, but
wasn't allowed to escape him. He opened the door for
her, and she almost ran to her car. It was just starting
to rain and with any luck she would be home before it
got heavy—and if she was quick she might just evade
the surgeon! Luckily she had her car keys in her hand
and had just turned the ignition when John grabbed
the car door.

They gazed at each other for a long moment, and
Claire almost relented when she saw the anguish in his
face. Then he shrugged. 'I'm not much good with
words, I'm afraid, and I seem to have made a mess of
my private life, as usual. There's no need to run from

me, Claire! If the prospect of marriage is that awful we won't pursue the mater. Goodnight, my dear — sleep well.' He strode away, and in the headlights Claire could see the rain glistening on his coat and bare head.

Even the skies are crying, she thought disconsolately as she reached the dark, empty house she had once thought of as home. The brisk wind was blowing the clouds away, but it couldn't blow away her misery. She loved him! Why on earth hadn't she accepted? Even though he didn't love her, they could have been happy together, surely? Yet he hated the idea of marriage — hadn't he said as much? And if he wasn't good with words, what was it he was trying to say? Those magic words 'I love you'?

She went all through the house, switching on every light in a futile effort to comfort herself. Then she sank down on the settee and gazed at the blank TV screen, unwilling even to make the effort to switch on. Suppose that *was* what he was trying to say, but years of unhappy marriage had stifled his ability to say them?

She jumped up. Yes, of course she would marry him! Gazing about her, Claire began to people the room with a family: there would be Katy, of course, and perhaps later on she would have the two brothers she'd invented! Whatever John might say about the girl's reasons for inventing 'the boys', Claire felt that Katy was lonely and would dearly love to have brothers or sisters. She obviously hated being the only one. And if John didn't like the idea, well. . . Claire smiled impishly at no one in particular. She would just have to use all her powers of persuasion, that was all!

Now. . . Was John at the Red House — or would he have gone back to the manor? That would be nearer for him and he'd said he had 'nearly' moved in — yes, he must be at the manor. As were all the Medhursts, *and* Katy. Claire's rosy glow faded. This called for some hard thinking. If you wanted something badly enough you had to reach out and grab it, not wait until it fell into someone else's hands. Or, in this case, into someone else's arms.

She went slowly up to her room, busily planning all the way. Wendy Clark was right, take your happiness while you could, and that was just what a certain Staff Nurse Shaw intended doing!

CHAPTER TWELVE

SISTER WHITELAW'S party was voted the success of the year, and Claire found herself singled out as the chief arranger of the party, receiving such fulsome praise that her cheeks burned before she had made even one circuit of the consultants' common-room.

The Camber Ward sister herself was surrounded by consultants, but Claire couldn't see John among their number. Probably he would appear once she had returned to Westfield, which, she saw, she must do in a few minutes to let Stella Pountney come in.

'Ah, Claire, isn't it?' a low, melodious voice said, as an elegantly slender hand reached for a glass of bitter lemon, Claire having been pressed into service as a soft-drinks waitress.

'Oh, hello, Miss Wallace. Yes, I'm Claire Shaw. I'm in your unit — at least —— ' Claire broke off, not knowing what to say to Katy's mother. The woman was smiling, though, so apparently hadn't heard about a certain evening's escapade!

'I hear you're responsible for organising this party. You must be fond of Sister Whitelaw,' Miss Wallace went on, her eyes fixed on Claire. 'It's always upsetting when one of the old guard retires. Then you will lose John,' she said, and Claire thought, I've already lost John, so what does it matter?

'Is Mr Colby coming this afternoon?' Claire tried to sound casual. 'I wouldn't want him to miss a glass of squash. We've nothing stronger, I'm afraid — Upstairs wouldn't allow it.'

Tania Wallace pulled a face. 'Typical of Upstairs, from what I hear! Never mind, I'll shake them up as much as John does! And yes, he *is* coming. In fact, he should be here by now. Katy wanted to come, too, but we persuaded her that it's a hospital-personnel-only function. She doesn't like to be left out of anything, you know.'

'Yes, I did know, actually,' Claire said bluntly, then wished the words unsaid, but Katy's fond mother merely smiled. Then, to Claire's amazement, she took the tray from her.

'You've done enough, Claire—enjoy the party for a while.' The surgeon went gliding away with the tray, which looked too heavy for her, and Claire was amused to see a tall young doctor hasten to relieve her of it. The sort of woman for whom strong men moved mountains! The thought tickled her funny bone, and she wondered whether John had been at Tania's beck and call. No, he wasn't the sort to walk to heel! Perhaps that was part of the trouble.

Tania Wallace came gliding back. 'There, that always happens!' she smiled. 'Now you and I are going to have a quiet talk, my dear. Let's go in search of a few crisps or something. There isn't much left, and I'm starving!'

Surprised, Claire said, 'There's some more in the kitchen—this way.' She took the initiative, easing a way through the throng for them, all the time wondering apprehensively what it was they were to have a 'quiet talk' about! Everything was going wrong. She'd had such high hopes of coming to an arrangement with John, but her good intentions of a few days before had come to nothing. Having been turned down once, he wasn't prepared even to discuss the matter. Oh, he was perfectly charming, as courteous as ever, but that warm smile had gone, the intense light in those blue, blue eyes, and it made her want to cry for what she had lost. Or, rather, for what she had never had so couldn't say she had actually lost—John's love.

Wendy hadn't helped, either. John had apppeared on Camber when Claire was paying one of her brief visits, and Wendy had thanked them both for making a sick woman happy. 'Name your first 'un after me, if you like!' she had added generously, and Claire hadn't known where to put her face. John's laughter still seemed to echo in her ears as she made room for his ex-wife in the spartan kitchen.

'We're a bit pushed for space, I'm afraid,' she apologised, 'but have a pew anyway.' Tania did as she was bid, seating herself on a hard chair, then eyed Claire composedly.

'I'm afraid Katy has been less than kind to you, Claire. She's been so determined to see John and me reunited, and herself part of a complete family, that she hasn't seen what's under her nose,' the surgeon began, and Claire couldn't pretend not to understand.

'Katy's lonely — she needs a family! Isn't there any chance of you and John getting back together?' Claire asked, hoping the answer would be *no*!

Tania smiled sadly. 'None whatsoever — I wouldn't have him back if he were the last man on earth! Katy realises that now. John and I staged a spectacular argument after he wined and dined us recently. Perhaps you saw us?'

'Yes, I did, but. . . *Why* wouldn't you have him back?' Claire asked indignantly, the slur on her beloved being one she couldn't let pass. 'He's a fine man, a good man, and. . .'

'And you love him. Yes, *I* understand that but does he? I agree that he's a fine man, but we simply weren't right for each other, Claire. We were two strong-minded people pulling in opposite directions, and neither of us would give way. I found my right partner with. . .' she hesitated briefly '. . .with Justin. Now I have to come to terms with that loss, but his sons think of me as a surrogate mother, even though they're teenagers, so that helps. After bereavement, the road's a long and hard one, but I'd like John to be as happy with you as I. . .' Tania's voice trailed off, and she half turned away, Claire's tender heart going out to her.

'John doesn't love me, and Wendy Clark's match-making embarrassed him,' Claire admitted. 'He doesn't think much of marriage. He said——' Belatedly she remembered she shouldn't be saying that to this particular person. 'I'll persuade him to change his mind,' she went on firmly. 'And I know why John *and*

Justin both loved you — you're not a bit the ogre we all expected!' she said cheerfully, but this time her blunder was deliberate, and she was pleased to hear Tania's soft laughter follow her as she made her way back to Westfield.

Now to search out a certain consultant! But the only person in the ward office was Stella Pountney, who eyed Claire without enthusiasm. 'Back, are you? I'd better put in an appearance.' She rose, then her expression softened a little. 'I hear congratulations are in order, Staff Nurse. Wendy's efforts haven't gone unrewarded. It's given her an interest and that's important to patients with cancer. I often think a determined will and a reason for living can help a lot.'

Knowing what this admission must have cost the woman, Claire didn't know what to say for a moment. Then she said, 'I wish you were right, but the idea was Wendy's, I'm afraid, not John's. He was annoyed by it all. . .' Her voice trailed away, and for a moment hope flared in the pale eyes opposite hers, then her senior brushed by, and Claire was left in charge. John was scattering broken hearts all over the place! And I'm one of them, she mused, then got on with the business of the day — the medicine round, then a quick check before visitors. *That* was what she was here for.

There was inevitably a quick turnover of patients on a surgical ward, and Claire just got used to the group of patients in one cubicle when they all changed, or so it seemed. Nurse Rees had given out the medication, and this left Claire free to do her usual round before evening visitors. Gram Collingwood had returned from the party, and he, somewhat surprisingly, offered to walk the ward with her.

'You've seen Mr Fisher, haven't you?' Claire began. 'He's for herniotomy. He's been wearing a truss but his GP's persuaded him that an operation is the real answer.'

'Yes, he's down for tomorrow, emergencies permitting. He didn't like being turfed out last year, you know. He developed a chest infection and we had to send him home. I hope he's OK this time.' He paused and gazed down at Claire, his expression more disapproving than usual. 'I hear you're putting in for Doris Whitelaw's job. Is that true?'

Gram sounded so amazed that Claire wanted to shake him.

'I wasn't going to, but. . .' She paused, then smiled sadly. 'I decided I had nothing to lose and much to gain, as they say! Why? I'm not exactly a beginner.' Claire gave the registrar what she hoped was a ward-sister-type smile.

'Sure, sure, don't get all fired up,' Gram said placatingly. 'It's just that I heard you and the chief were getting hitched, or shacking up together — opinions vary — and I was surprised you should want the sister's job, that's all.'

'You can tell the grapevine that I'm not doing either — marrying *or* shacking up with John,' Claire said, holding on to her temper with difficulty. Gram would try the patience of a saint but John thought highly of him so she must try—— Oh, bother what John thought!

By now they were in what had been George Upshall's cubicle, but he had been discharged that morning. He was still a sick man but he and his wife were facing the future bravely, and Mrs Upshall had promised to let Claire know how her husband got on at John's outpatients clinic. In his place was the herniotomy patient, Bob Fisher, whom Gram had already assessed. Next to him was Archie O'Neill, a big, cheerful man who was to go down for an operation on his colon the following morning.

Mr O'Neill would need a colostomy bag afterwards, and Gram spent some time going over the explanation John had already given the man. Claire sat quietly listening, realising now the truth of the night nurse's words: John had made Gram more human, more aware of patients as *people*. Even if he left now, he would be leaving a more understanding registrar behind. Oh, no — he couldn't leave! Not without her.

She became aware that the more understanding registrar was glaring at her and had obviously spoken without her hearing him. 'I'm sorry, Mr Collingwood?' she said guiltily.

'I was saying, Staff Nurse, that Mr O'Neill still hasn't met anyone else who's had a similar operation. Can you arrange something, please?'

No, Gram hadn't changed that much. Claire rose. 'Yes, of course. We've two patients lined up to have a chat to you, Mr O'Neill.' Claire gave him her sunny smile. 'One's just been discharged from another ward but he's promised to come in this evening. And Mr Turner will be in just as soon as I can get him over from Rotherfield Ward.'

It was important for prospective colostomy patients to meet those who'd had a similar operation, and had not only survived but had learned to cope well with the bag. In addition, a specially trained stoma nurse visited all such patients before operation, to explain the difficulties that might arise afterwards and how they could be overcome. Claire had found that the question that bothered most patients was the smell and the fear of giving offence to others, but that, too, could be dealt with easily.

'Did you see that Mrs Plumpton's back in Camber?' Gram muttered as she escorted him to the next cubicle.

'I've been in to see her,' Claire affirmed. 'Apparently her husband's back with her. Let's hope he doesn't go again just before her op!'

They had two vacancies now on Westfield, both booked, but if Claire had thought John might look in on the ward before he left she was to be disappointed. She heard from one of the other nurses that he had put in a brief appearance at the party but left the hospital immediately afterwards. It underlined his determination not to be browbeaten into marrying a certain nurse, anyway, and another arrow pierced Claire's poor heart.

At this rate she could set up in business as professional target, she thought morosely as she prepared to go off duty. Worse still, in a few days' time Suzanne was throwing a big engagement party at the house, and Claire didn't know how she would be able to cope

with the heartache. For her cousin's sake she would
put on a brilliant smile, toast the happy couple, wish
them well in the New World, but it wouldn't be easy.

Then the telephone rang and she reached for it, just
as the night staff appeared. 'Hello, Westfield Ward,
Staff Nurse Shaw, can I——?' she began, but wasn't
allowed to finish.

'Hello, Staff Nurse Shaw, this is Miss Katy Colby
speaking,' a young voice said. 'I'm sorry to disturb
you, but Daddy says can you meet him at the Red
House on your way home? It's very urgent—thank
you.'

The line went dead, nd an exasperated Claire put
the receiver down. What was Katy up to now? And
what was so important that John had to send a message
via his daughter? It smelled fishy, but perhaps he was
afraid of a rebuff and had asked Katy to mediate. No.
Claire shook her head. That didn't ring true either.
Yet it was a chance to see John again, to talk to him,
and she wasn't about to turn down that chance.

Nor was she about to fling herself at his head, Claire
decided as she neared Hemsley Green a few minutes
later. Whatever he had to say, she would listen, and
that would be that. She had her pride, too. Wasn't it
John who had said people took advantage of her kind
heart? Now he was doing the very same thing!

There were no lights on at the Red House when she
stopped the car, and she hesitated about getting out
since it looked as if John wasn't even there. But
perhaps there was a light around the back. . .

There wasn't, and Claire hesitated briefly before
dashing up to the front door and ringing the bell
several times, then hammering on the door, much as
Katy had done. No, she definitely wasn't going to
linger in the dark! Then she recalled John's words
about Katy fearing he'd fallen through a rotting floorboard. No—surely the agents wouldn't have taken the
property on if the house was in such a poor state?

No, of course they wouldn't. They couldn't have
tenants falling into the basement! But the Red House
was old, and, remembering the creaky stairs and the

uneven steps at the rear of the house, Claire's imagination went into overdrive. John could be lying unconscious somewhere!

Shivering in the cool evening air and wishing she weren't wearing a summer dress and thin jacket, Claire gazed about her uneasily. Of course there was nothing to fear in the village. Hadn't she run all the way home in the dark that never-to-be-forgotten night? But she hadn't been running from a dark, empty house then.

Berating herself for abject cowardice, Claire went all the way around the house, peering in such windows as she could and tapping on each one as she passed. Finally she ended up at the back door and hammered on that until her knuckles ached, before listening for any sounds the injured John might make.

Then she heard a stealthy, slithering sort of noise, and she panicked, calling out, 'John? Is that you?' before running back to the comforting bulk of her Mini. What a fool he would think her if he could see her now, she thought. But he must be here! Why else should Katy send her to. . .? Realisation dawned — Katy! Was this a prank? Or something deeper — a way to get back at her parents for not wanting to remarry? A way to get back at *me* for daring to fall in love with Daddy, Claire corrected herself. Yet she couldn't be sure. The obvious thing to do was drive home and ring the manor from there, and she could have kicked herself for not thinking of that before.

Panic and anxiety drive all sensible thoughts from a patient's head, she told herself as she got into the car. Then she was caught in the glare from a set of headlights as a car negotiated the carriage sweep. The lights were dipped and she saw it was the Mercedes. John!

'Claire! What are you doing here?' He got out of his car and just stared for a moment.

Claire was cold, tired, and rther hungry, and *he* had the nerve to ask her that! 'You sent for me urgently, so here I am. What are you up to?' she countered. 'I've been tapping on the windows, calling through the letterbox, hammering on the door. . .'

The unsmiling surgeon came striding towards her, crossing the welcome pool of light. 'I've just been to the District but they told me you'd left. I thought I was dreaming when I saw you here,' he went on slowly. 'And what was that about tapping on the windows? There's no one else here!'

Ignoring that, Claire asked, 'Why the District?' *Was* all this Katy's doing—sending her father to the hospital and herself to this deserted house? No, that would be too petty of the girl. Katy wasn't like that, and Claire dismissed the charges she'd brought against her!

'Because you're usually late leaving and I thought I would catch you there,' John was saying slowly, his gaze intent. 'We can't talk out here—come in and I'll make us some coffee.'

The prospect of coffee was immensely appealing, particularly after her vivid imaginings of the past few minutes, and Claire willingly followed him through to the kitchen. 'Autumn's coming,' she commented, more for something to say than anything else, as she felt awkward now.

John's gaze was thoughtful as it rested upon her. 'Yes, autumn's coming and I'll be gone soon, though I'm keeping the house on for weekends. Tania says she's about to return, so. . .' He turned on the tap. 'Look out a couple of mugs, will you, please? There's an assortment over there—Katy's been stocking me up. How did you come to be here, anyway?'

Claire hesitated. 'I had a phone call from Katy. She said you wanted me to come here, that it was urgent—so I came. And what did I find? A cold, empty, rather spooky house, with you probably lying somewhere unconscious! I called to you, and tapped, and. . .and there was this horrid slithering noise,' she remembered suddenly. Yes, now *that* hadn't been her imagination.

'I wasn't aware I made horrid slithering noises, Staff Nurse, but we'll investigate while the coffee's heating. Where was it?' Taking her hand, he gazed quizzically down at her, his touch warming her far more than a coffee would have done.

'It was by the back door. It's probably nothing,'

Claire admitted, ashamed now of her panic attack. 'I'll show you.'

Hand in hand, they walked through the house, and John opened the rear door and peered out. For a moment there was silence, though Claire could hear the wind rising. Then the slithery noise came again in a gust of wind, this time followed by an eerie tapping, and John chuckled, his shoulders heaving. 'Look.' He pointed to the upstairs window, where a branch from the wild roses had begun slithering across the glass again. 'Something we'll have to get pruned,' he murmured, laughter in his voice.

'What made you decide I was unconscious? Surely that wasn't another of Katy's vivid imaginings?' he asked once they were back in the kitchen and Claire could bring herself to laugh at her fear of an unpruned rambling rose.

'No, it was one of my own,' she had to admit. 'I thought you might have fallen through one of those rotting floorboards Katy was worried about!' Their shared laughter was therapeutic, the more so when he took her in his arms. Claire laid her head against his comforting shoulder for a moment, before looking up. 'What was Katy up to? Why send you to the hospital and me here?'

'No, she didn't. She knew I was here earlier, but she couldn't have known I'd take it into my head to go haring off to the District in search of my future wife! She was doing what she could to bring us together, not fling us apart, my love. Anyway, I've moved in now but she's remaining with the Medhursts — they've offered to keep her and Dandy until I get a house-keeper lined up. Let's have that coffee, hmm?'

Claire clasped her cold hands around the mug John handed her, his words only now sinking in. 'What was that about a future wife, sir?' she asked innocently, and he smiled that slow, sensuous smile she had first seen on the face of the unshaven stranger in the Medhursts' garden.

'I decided that Wendy's idea was a good one, though I've been fighting the attraction ever since I met a sapphire-eyed nymph in the manor garden! I enjoyed being a bachelor dad, and Katy protected me from predatory females. I thought I could get off lightly, that you and I could have an affair, live in London maybe. . .then part amicably in due course. Remain friends, as Tania and I have done all this time, but. . .' He shrugged, then grinned boyishly. 'My selfish ideas came to nothing. I couldn't get the tender-hearted, sapphire-eyed nymph out of my mind! Will you marry me, Sapphire Eyes? I have it on the best authority that I'm impossible to live with, obsessional about my work, in love with my computer. . . Let me see now, was there anything else? Tania made out a whole list of my faults and showed it to Katy, just to prove her point, but there may have been a few more I've forgotten!' John gazed at her intently for a moment, as if aware of her silence. 'Well?' he demanded. 'Will you?'

'I was wondering whether I had any choice,' Claire said sweetly, enjoying the humour of the situation.

'No, not really,' he admitted. 'But you haven't said you will, Claire. Look. . .' he leaned forward across the table so that their hands touched, and Claire closed her eyes for a few seconds, waves of longing sweeping over her '. . .I know I've got all the faults that Tania spoke about, but I'm clean and tidy, house-trained, and. . . Claire?' he said almost pleadingly, when she didn't speak. 'Is it still Martin?' His voice had hardened, and Claire looked at him in astonishment. She had forgotten Martin!

'Oh, no! I hope he and his wife can sort out their problems. I'd forgotten him,' she admitted. 'Isn't that awful?'

'What about when we made love, Claire? You obviously remembered him *then*.' There was hurt in John's eyes now, and Claire wanted to cry.

'Not the way you think! I. . . I was so pleased because you didn't turn me away, leave me afterwards. That you wanted to lie with me in that awful bed,' she said with a little smile. 'Martin. . .he never did,' she went on slowly. 'He would reach for his cigarettes, and

I told him once that he had to give up smoking, or give me up. And eventually he did both. That's what I meant when I said I was thinking about Martin. Male-like, you must have supposed I was comparing lovers!' she went on, tartly, and John grinned, the hurt expression disappearing as if it had never been.

'Just because it's Wendy's dearest wish, you don't *have* to marry me, you know. I don't expect it,' Claire said hesitantly, anxious to give him a way out if he wanted one, needing him to be sure this time. She couldn't bear a broken marriage.

John glanced down at their clasped hands. 'I fought against it, against you, but Staff Nurse Shaw defeated me in the end, her kindness, her warm, caring nature, her love. . .'

'If I thought you cared about me, just a little, I *might* consider your proposition,' Claire said, relenting.

'Claire!' John jumped up, pulled back the table, then swung one astonished nurse up into his arms. 'Did I forget to tell you I love you? That must be another of my faults!' he went on, his breath warm against her ear, the loving expression in his eyes telling Claire all she needed to know.

Then she snuggled closer, all her dreams coming true at long last. 'Tell me again,' she demanded.

When their first son was born, Mr and Mrs Colby couldn't make up their minds whether to call him Robert or Johnnie, so it was left to Katy to choose. Katy, the harum-scarum pre-teen, was now a boy-conscious teenager and her particular idol was named Johnnie, so that solved the problem.

'Of course, we could have tossed a coin,' John murmured against Claire's ear as they gazed enrap-tured at their baby. 'Next time it must be Robert's turn!'

'Next time we shall have a Wendy,' Claire said firmly. And they did.

LOVE ON CALL
4 FREE BOOKS AND 2 FREE GIFTS

F R O M   M I L L S   &   B O O N

Capture all the drama and emotion of a hectic medical world when
you accept 4 Love on Call romances PLUS a cuddly teddy bear and a
mystery gift - absolutely FREE and without obligation. And, if you
choose, go on to enjoy 4 exciting Love on Call romances every
month for only £1.80 each! Be sure to return the coupon below today
to: Mills & Boon Reader Service, FREEPOST, PO Box 236,
Croydon, Surrey CR9 9EL.

— — — — — **NO STAMP REQUIRED** — — — — — —

YES! Please rush me 4 FREE Love on Call books and 2 FREE gifts! Please
also reserve me a Reader Service subscription, which means I can look
forward to receiving 4 brand new Love on Call books for only £7.20 every
month, postage and packing FREE. If I choose not to subscribe, I shall write to
you within 10 days and still keep my FREE books and gifts. I may cancel or
suspend my subscription at any time. I am over 18 years. Please write in
BLOCK CAPITALS.

Ms/Mrs/Miss/Mr _____ **EP63D**

Address _____

_____

Postcode _____ Signature _____

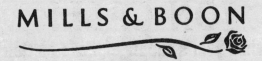

ON CALL!
Win a year's supply of 'Love on Call' romances ABSOLUTELY FREE?

Yes, you can win one whole year's supply of 'Love on Call' romances! It's easy! All you have to do is convert the four sets of numbers below into television soaps by using the letters in the telephone dial. Fill in your answers plus your name and address details overleaf, cut out and send to us by 30th Sept. 1994.

1 5233315767 _____

2 3552 152 1819 _____

3 165547322 _____

4 2177252267 _____

Please turn over for entry details

ON CALL!

SEND YOUR ENTRY NOW!

The first five correct entries picked out of the bag after the closing date will each win one year's supply of 'Love on Call' romances (four books every month - worth over £85). What could be easier?

Don't forget to enter your name and address in the space below then put this page in an envelope and post it today (you don't need a stamp). Competition closes 30th Sept. '94.

> **'Love on Call' Competition**
> **FREEPOST**
> **P.O. Box 236**
> **Croydon**
> **Surrey CR9 9EL**

EPLQ

Are you a Reader Service subscriber?   Yes ☐   No ☐

Ms/Mrs/Miss/Mr _____

Address _____

_____

_____

Postcode _____

Signature

_____